Christian's Walk
The Journey

Inspired by the immortal classic *Pilgrim's Progress* by John Bunyan

Written and Illustrated by Jack Billups

Now to the King eternal, immortal, invisible,
the only God, be honor and glory forever and ever,
Amen.

1 Timothy 1:17

Copyright © 2022 Jack Billups
All rights reserved.
ISBN:9781736037669

"All Rights Reserved. No part of this publication may be reproduced, distributed, or transmitted in any form or by any means, or stored in a database or retrieval system, without written permission of the author."

Table of Contents

Introduction _____ 1
1 The Last Mile _____ 5
2 Destruction City _____ 9
3 The Journey Begins _____ 19
4 The Gate _____ 31
5 The Old House _____ 37
6 The Burden Falls _____ 47
7 Strange Encounters _____ 61
8 A Confrontation _____ 77
9 An Old Friend _____ 89
10 Deep Discoveries _____ 101
11 Vanity Fair _____ 113
12 Strange Encounters _____ 133
13 Giant Despair _____ 143
14 Just Delectable _____ 155
15 Family Reunion _____ 165
16 Snared _____ 175
17 The Resting Lodge _____ 183
18 And May Enter _____ 193

Introduction

John Bunyan's immortal classic, *Pilgrim's Progress,* has been retold countless times throughout the ages. The changes in time, culture, and language have created the need to share Bunyan's story again.

John Bunyan 1628 - 1688

Bunyan was a character given to fluent profanity, other worldly pursuits, and various questionable games. He married a godly young woman whose life and testimony must have profoundly influenced him. Finally, John repented of his sins and came to Christ. Born again, Bunyan became a new man, quickly abandoning his old ways.

He was a Tinker by trade, a mender of pots and pans. After his conversion, John began openly sharing his faith in Christ while supporting his family. Bunyan became popular among the ordinary people of his day as he preached the *Good News* with vigor and conviction.

He rebelled against the formal traditions of the established church, which demanded his attendance to sit and listen and not to be preaching. But, of course, this was impossible with John's knowledge of the scriptures.

So, he was subsequently arrested and thrown in jail for his insistence on sharing Christ and refusing to attend church. He spent the next twelve years in Bedford Jail except for a few brief intervals of freedom. His ceaseless study of the Bible while in prison and his sharp perception of the human heart gave him wisdom and insight. This was reflected in the unique format he created when he began writing *Pilgrim's Progress.*

After his release, John's book became a best seller and a coveted possession of America's early settlers. *The Bible* and *Pilgrim's Progress* were the two books loved and read by most Christians for three hundred years. *Pilgrim's Progress* succeeded in conveying the Bible's truths, exhortations, promises, warnings, and guidance, putting it within the intellectual grasp of regular people.

Pilgrim's Progress is still as appropriate as ever, and powerfully effective, bringing non-believers to the Cross and believers closer to Jesus.

Christian's Walk adapts Bunyan's classic to our current tumultuous world, making it understandable and relevant, just as Bunyan did in his day.

Why Jack Billups?

In the winter of my *Journey*, I have a vault of experiences and insights. Therefore, I created my version using my imagination for new characters, circumstances, and dialogues.

In 1970, I returned home from that crazy Asian war, Vietnam. Although I attended church as a boy, my faith was on the back burner. Like John Bunyan, I, too, engaged in reckless behavior.

Soon, an old friend from the neighborhood visited; however, Jesus Christ came with him, and remained with me. My friend, Sammy, took the time to explain that I could be forgiven of my sins and have a living relationship with Jesus Christ.

"Behold, I stand at the door and knock; if anyone hears My voice and opens the door, I will come into him and will dine with him, and he with Me." *Revelations 3:20*

That's precisely what I did; I opened the door and let Him in. So now, Christ dwells in me, comforting, guiding, and keeping me in His will.

Several weeks passed when I met an English missionary couple, Ted and Milley Ware. This precious couple was in their senior years and now traveled around the States in their humble camper.

While serving as missionaries in Cuba in the mid-fifties, Ted and Millie traveled down a road and into an ambush by Castro revolutionaries. Unfortunately, they were mistaken for the enemy, and shots were fired in their direction. Ted was hit in the face, and although they survived the attack, Ted and Milley returned to the United States. Sadly, their days as missionaries in Cuba were over. Ted lost one eye and wore a black patch, which added character to his already animated persona.

Ted and Millie came to my neighborhood to visit mutual friends. The Kelley family was caring and helped me grow in The Lord. While living in their quaint camper, Ted and I spent endless hours together, creating evangelical tracts, *Tee Jay Publications*. Then eventually, a book, *The Late Great Pilgrim's Progress.*

Even back in the seventies, the need existed to adapt *Pilgrim's Progress* into a format much easier to comprehend. So, with Ted's colorful expression ability and spiritual insights, he began refurbishing his fellow Englishman's story. My part was to help develop the storyline and create the artwork. Finally, in 1973 we launched *The Late Great Pilgrim's Progress.* Ted and I enjoyed a real sense of accomplishment.

Ted and Millie's *Journeys* have ended, and they are with the

Lord. So now, fifty years removed from that chapter of my life, I've decided to do it again, this time by myself, both writing and illustrations.

Much of Ted Ware's writing remains. However, I have modified, expanded, and created new characters and their stories. Therefore, I present *Christian's Walk: The Journey* by Jack Billups with fresh eyes and a unique perspective. This adaptation could only be formed in times such as these.

Chapter 1
The Last Mile

Christian reaches the knoll's crest with a final gasp for air. The old wooden marker on the side read *One More Mile.*

Indeed, this has been a long *journey;* although joyful, Christian is now old and weary. Surrounded by fields of autumn colors, reds, oranges, and yellows sway as the wind freely stirs God's creation into a beautiful live painting. This enters his eyes and prompts him to say, "Thank You, Lord."

Looking down at the last mile of this path, in full view, he sees what he has known for so long; his *journey* will end at the *River of Death*. Christian has no choice; he must move on and step into its cold, dark waters.

But before continuing, it's time to pause. In the grass, Christian sees a comfortable-looking chair. This chair must be the *Chair of Reflection* that waits at the end of everyone's *journey.* "Christian, sit and rest," a voice whispers, so he complies.

While settling into this soft, warm chair, he looks north across the *River of Death;* the trail continues on the other side, causing his heart to leap. Christian ponders more intently*: I see everything differently, like a transparent vision floating in and out; however, it's real!* The trail continues upward on the river's other side, where oscillations of vivid colors are flashing beyond.

Knowing he will arrive soon at this long-awaited place of beauty; Christian decides to spend his final hours looking back on his life. He returns to the images and feelings of a time gone by. With a strange mixture of joy and sadness, he tearfully relives the events of his life as a young boy.

Then, Christian began reflecting on the many funerals of family elders who have slipped into eternity.

Christian wondered; *Can it be that the Lord has prepared a place for everyone who dies?* Knowing that some in his family were hostile to God, Chris questioned the pronouncements of the officiating ministers. Instead, they, without truly understanding, comforted the family, saying that one day they would reunite with their loved ones in Heaven. Chris knew nothing of God's *Way* to Heaven; however, something in his gut told him, *How can everyone enter Heaven when they die?*

Then Christian reflected on times past with his wife and children. *Did I give them enough time and love? Did I discourage my children? Was I too strict? Was I tender and kind to my wife, or did I try to show her who the boss was?*

These questions and many others raced through *Christian's* mind knowing he could not return and do things differently. The truth: *Christian* was a perceptive and gentle soul who did his best to become the priest of his home.

Days before, Christian said his final farewells to his family. Although sad, he comforts himself, knowing they will be together for eternity. Christian raised his family to love God and travel only in *His Way*.

Having exhausted his memories, Christian notices movement on the trail below. *Could this be my old friend Grateful? However, two people were walking. So, I must wait and see.*

Early in Christian's *journey,* he traveled with another friend named *Faithful*. Christian longs to see him again; however, *Faithful* encountered a tragedy along *The Way.* Like-minded, they shared the same *frustrations* in their hometown, *Destruction City. Faithful* decided first to seek *The Truth.* Then, later on, Christian made his decision and started his *journey*.

Time passed, and finally, they found each other walking in the same direction.

Christian and *Faithful* went through some crazy times, always encouraging each other to keep going. However, the most trying experience was when they exited a thickly wooded section of a forest and came upon a village in the distance. "This must be *Vanity Fair,*" commented Christian. "I believe you're right," said *Faithful*. Many on the *journey* have passed down horrendous stories of those who traveled through *Vanity Fair.* Their warnings have been clear; guard your hearts and minds, and those who don't suffer greatly!"

Even from a distance, they could tell this was an immoral place by the advertisement billboards polluting the landscape along the way. Unfortunately, the path took Christian and *Faithful* right into the bowels of this God-forsaken place. They both girded up in preparation, making sure their *Breastplates* and *Swords* were polished.

The events in *Vanity Fair* altered their courses along *The Way*; they became separated. Christian muses, *we went through some crazy adventures together.*

Bringing himself back to the present, Christian decides, *I will rest and spend what little time I have left soaking in His creation.* The breeze cools him as he reclines in peace.

Why is it now that I see everything so clearly? The colors are vivid and bright, and the birds swoop up and down, singing. The trees reach towards the heavens as if they are praising God; perhaps they are, although in a language we don't comprehend., I don't understand why so many people don't see this.

The Big Book is correct; **Having eyes, do you not see? And having ears, do you not hear?** Mark 8;18

Once again, Christian's mind returns to the beginning of his journey. He recalls his alienation from his wife and friends when he began seeking the *Way*. So much has happened between then and now. And soon, eternity will begin!

The *journeyer's* arrive at the hilltop, huffing and puffing. Christian lifts his head, and makes eye contact.

Christian Reflects on His Life

Chapter 2
Destruction City

"Turn off the TV!" shouted Chris. Extremely frustrated, he raced from the house, mumbling, "I can't believe this; the world has gone collectively insane. Nothing makes sense anymore. Everything right is wrong, and everything wrong, is now right. Our leaders are no longer leaders but weak, self-indulging frauds, only looking out for themselves. Everyone is looking out for themselves! Whatever happened to courtesy, kindness, and integrity? Now it's fashionable to disrespect seniors, boastfully spew profanities, and see who can push the furthest boundaries of decency and modesty! Why does my culture celebrate perversion and lewdness? Why are criminals pitied while their victims are ignored? My kids haven't a chance!"

Chris left the house shaking his head and crossed the street into a lush park featuring grand oak trees and thick vegetation, a beautiful place to escape life's stresses. Finding a bench, he sat and continued his thoughts.

What's it all about? Nothing has meaning, and here I am with my wife and kids; no future, no nothing. Nothing, just an empty feeling. Nothing satisfies, and nothing gratifies. God! At my time of life too! Everything to live for, yet nothing to look forward to but Destruction. Yes, that's what this place is, Destruction! It's like a cloud of darkness covering the earth's atmosphere raining down storms of dissension, division, envy, hatred, and depravity on the human race. Families are being destroyed, creating a wake of disillusioned children: nothing but bad news all the time. The only mention of Good News was spoken to me one Saturday afternoon after a grueling week at the office.

Chris Contemplates

Chris walked to a popular outside bar near home. Secluded behind hills, this was the perfect place for the herd of similar frustrated people to come and collectively numb their pain and loneliness. Sitting alone and sipping on a Bloody Mary, Chris felt the ground beneath begin to vibrate. Then, like rolling thunder, a biker gang rumbled in, lots of them! Becoming uncomfortable, Chris attempted to keep from looking at them; however, no such luck. Instead, they filed in front of the park bench where Chris was seated; many of them made eye contact, smiled, and said, "Hi, how are you doing?"

What a strange lot, Chris thought. Mostly older men and women sporting tattoos, long hair, beards, bandannas, Levi's, and boots. They seemed friendly enough, making Chris relieved, and then he noticed the group's name on the backside of their leather vests, *Bikers for Jesus.* Chris laughed and whispered, "I've seen it all!"

Now distracted from his problems, Chris observed this unusual family for entertainment. They sat at a picnic table while laughing, talking, and patting one another on the back. Several went as far as giving one another hugs. Noticeable and unexpected was the conduct that surfaced. They weren't dropping "F" bombs, and they were polite.

Moreover, when the waitress approached, it stood out that they ordered water instead of booze. *Wow, what are they doing here? Shouldn't they be in church having a Bible study?*

Suddenly, one jumped up and walked by Chris toward the motorcycles, then returned holding a Big Black Book. *Oh my God, did I do that?* Chris questioned himself. The man returned to his people, opened his *Book,* and read aloud. *This guy is bold; he must be their leader,* concluded Chris. Then he rose and walked in Chris's direction holding his Big Black Book.

Enjoying his Bloody Mary buzz, Chris wondered, *Is he coming to me?* Sure enough, he did. "Hi, my name is Jimmy; I noticed you're alone, so I came to say Hello."

"Hi Jimmy, my name is Chris, short for Christian, have a seat. Yeah, I'm unwinding from work before returning home to the wife and kids; you know how that goes. Your biker's club is a bit unconventional!"

Jimmy laughed, then explained to Chris that the group often come here to enjoy food and fellowship.

Then Chris asked, "Are you their leader?"

"Well, I'm a pastor who rides with the club."

Chris's curiosity was piqued, and he began asking Pastor Jimmy about his life. Pastor Jimmy graciously shared his roles and responsibilities along with some fascinating stories. He told Chris he was called to be with those in hospitals soon to die. Jimmy shared that he had been to murders and suicides to pray and be available to comfort those in despair.

After hearing these remarkable stories, Chris said, "You certainly don't look like a conventional pastor. Do you ever wear a suit and tie?"

Jimmy responded with a grin between his incredibly long gray mustache, "Nope!" Then, Pastor Jimmy asked, "So, Chris, what are you unwinding from?"

Feeling relaxed now, Chris shared his frustrations with the Pastor. Jimmy listened intently without interruption. After Chris got it all out, Pastor Jimmy consoled him and shared some surprising details about his past and the burden he carried for many years. Chris reacted. "You were a druggie?"

"I sure was!" The Pastor affirmed. "Not only did I use drugs, but I sold them to support my addiction, but not anymore."

Pastor Jimmy told Chris about *a Way, a Path, a Straight* and *Narrow Trail* that leads to *The Truth*. He continued. "And on this *Path*, there's a place where you can remove that backpack you carry."

Now puzzled, Chris asked, "What backpack?"

Pastor Jimmy explained: "It's the weight of guilt and shame from the lies, rebellion, selfishness, hate, bitterness, and resentment you've accumulated throughout your life. In a nutshell, it's called sin, and it's a heavy burden to carry, and I

Pastor Jimmy & Chris

guess that's why you're here now, hoping to feel better."

By now, the bikers were leaving, walking toward Chris and Jimmy. The Pastor stood and said, "Chris, let me pray for you." Chris nodded, so Jimmy laid his hand on Chris's shoulder and prayed.

Then, Pastor Jimmy said. "Goodbye, Chris; I hope you begin your *journey*. Take this Big Black Book; it will guide you along *The Way*."

Feeling good about their conversation, Chris replied, "Thanks, Pastor Jimmy, it's been good talking with you."

With that, these *Bikers for Jesus* got on their bikes and rumbled away, leaving a cloud of dust in their wake. Chris thought: *that was a unique encounter, but it all felt right.*

Then, Chris came back to the present, sitting in the park. *That's it; none of this is a coincidence; I must make a move! I can no longer endure this restlessness. I will find The Way to release my burdens!*

Gazing north through the trees, he noticed the beginning of a trail that reached the horizon. But, what he saw appeared translucent. Not sure what to make of it, Chris turned around and walked back home. He approached his wife, Angela, who was washing the dishes. Chris asked her to join him on the front porch. After both settled in, Angela smiled at Chris and asked, "What's up Honey? Is something bothering you?"

So, Christian opened up and shared his struggles, frustrations, and longing to find answers. He told her about his conversation with Pastor Jimmy. Immediately, Angela's countenance changed to scorn and disapproval. Chris held up the Big Black Book and said, "The Pastor told me that all the answers to life are here." Angela glared at her husband, stood up, and marched back into the house.

Rejection swept over Chris as he hung his head and began processing his dilemma. Angela *and I are going in different directions; now what?* The romance, consideration, and tenderness waned after years of raising their children and paying bills. All this, plus their stress at work, and their attempts to get ahead, drained the joy and excitement from their relationship.

Although his heart ached, Chris's hunger for what Pastor Jimmy and his biker friends possessed was stronger than his alienation from Angela. He became more determined to follow through in his search for *The Truth*. Chris concluded; *succeeding in my journey may save our marriage and family.* He entered the house with resolve and walked into the bedroom. Angela rose from the bed and glared at him. Nothing was said, Chris turned around, entered the living

Chris and Angela

room, and lay on the sofa. He eked out a whisper of a prayer, "God, if you exist, please help me," and then he fell asleep.

A new day began, and it didn't take long for the fire of gossip to spread throughout the neighborhood. So, the concerned citizens of *Destruction City* marched over to Chris's doorstep to rescue him from his foolishness. But, while reasoning with Chris, they became angry. Several neighbors laughed with disgust, telling him not to be stupid. However, the worst was a tall, tight-jawed man named *Obstinate*. With squinted eyes, he locked onto Chris and began hurling verbal arrows at him without mercy, calling him a deceived idiot. Finally, *Obstinate* spun around with his chin up and stormed off the porch.

Not liking their insults and attempts to discourage him, Chris told the crowd, "I will do just what Pastor Jimmy said. I'm going to seek this *Way.*" So, the rest walked off, shaking their heads in disgust.

Chris was shaken. He experienced a host of emotions at that moment. *They wouldn't let me get a word in, and so much for friends supporting friends!* Disappointment, hurt, and anger fueled Chris's determination to begin the *journey.*

Angela continued being belligerent; she resisted her husband's new aspiration. Chris attempted to comfort her, then said, "Honey, I'm not leaving you; this is an inward, *spiritual,* and *heart journey.* I need answers, peace, and purpose, and I won't find it by going in circles daily, wallowing in frustration."

Angela returned to the house, leaving her distraught husband on the porch.

Chris noticed one friend, *Pliable,* remained on the swing bench behind him. Now, *Pliable* was different; he allowed that he'd like to find it if there was a *Way.* But one minute, he was up, and the next, down.

Pliable asked. "Do you think that Book has a message?"

Chris and *Pliable* were tight friends and grew up together in the same neighborhood. They tried out all the current trends and fads, but there was always a letdown after every form of induced excitement. At times, Chris and *Pliable* would discuss deep philosophical topics, admitting there must be something more. But they could never find a satisfactory answer. So, Chris took a seat to talk about the *journey.* Finally, a decision was reached; *Pliable* would join Christian on *The Way.*

Friends Set Chris Straight

Angela was eavesdropping, then, hearing their decision, she returned to the porch to scold her husband and *Pliable*. "I've seen you two experiment with many new and crazy things together, and now you will become religious fanatics! Let me know when you can admit you've gone off the deep end!"

Chris answered his wife's discouraging remarks. "Angela, this is genuine; let's do this together!"

She shook her head. "No!" then stormed back into the house.

Chris hung his head, then told *Pliable,* "Go home and prepare.

We'll head out tomorrow morning at sunup." Chris entered the house and made some sandwiches for the journey.

Fearful it would be another long night, he climbed into bed.

Angela was on the other side, with her back facing her husband. Chris whispered, "Goodnight, honey, I love you," but she did not respond.

Morning arrived. Chris and *Pliable* walked off the porch toward the park. As soon as they entered the park, a transformation occurred. Something Pastor Jimmy said came to mind: **Seek, and you will find.** *Matthew 7:7* Chris was surrounded by a world not seen by physical eyes, a reality not subject to time, a realm where invisible powers existed. Chris became aware that what Pastor Jimmy spoke to him was real. He hoped his wife would change her mind and begin her journey to discover *The Truth*.

Chapter 3
The Journey Begins

Chris and *Pliable* disappeared on the trail that began at the park's edge. "Hurry up," *Pliable* demanded. Already exhausted, Chris shot back, "I'm trying, but this weight on my back is slowing me down."

Then *Pliable* peppered Chris with questions. "What do you think is ahead of us?"

Chris paused to think, then said. "I can't tell you, but if the Pastor is right, I can look forward to dropping our burdens, getting answers about life, and experiencing peace.

Pliable, not satisfied, replied. "Well, I hope this journey will be fun, I haven't had a thrill for a long time!"

Chris quietly questioned *Pliable's* expectations and motives, then responded, "We'll just have to wait and see. In the meantime, we need to keep moving forward."

Both turned into their thoughts. Now concerned about *Pliable's* reason for coming, Chris thinks. *If Pliable is just looking for a new experience that stimulates him, I don't believe he will find The Truth.*

"I'm starving," sputtered *Pliable*.

Chris agreed, "Me too, let's stop for lunch."

They sat on large boulders under some oak trees. The creek nearby provided fresh, cool water to drink and clean off the sweat. "I packed some food for the journey," announced Chris.

Pliable extended his hand for a scrumptious-looking tuna sandwich and an apple. "Thanks, Chris! "While they

Pliable

ate and rested, they reminisced about the "good ole days" that really weren't that good. First, they recalled how they followed the crowds into risky behavior, always ending in a train wreck. Then, they remembered how they buckled, fearing rejection if they didn't join the others experiencing the latest trends.

"I can't believe we survived all that foolishness," Chris remarked.

Then *Pliable* sounded off. "You must admit, we had a lot of fun!" Chris rolled his eyes and thought, *Knucklehead*. Many of Chris and *Pliable's* peers suffered grave consequences while others perished, having crossed boundaries into addictions and immoral behaviors.

Chris made a final comment. "It's regretful that we have wasted so many years because of our foolish choices. But

Pastor Jimmy mentioned that something would happen along *The Way*. He read to me from his Big Black Book; **I will make up to you for the years that the swarming locust has eaten.** *Joel 2:25* An awesome way of saying that God will restore the years we've wasted away. That's why I'm on the path, *Pliable!*"

"Sounds cool to me. Come on, Chris, let's get going!"

Now refreshed and encouraged, they headed out into a dense portion of the woods. It became cold and hard to see.

"Chris!" *Pliable* shouted, "I'm going back; I forgot my jacket."

"Hang in there, *Pliable*," responded Chris, "we will find a place to camp for the night and start a fire." *Pliable* hung his head and continued. The sun sank behind the mountains, making it difficult to see. Then, suddenly, the earth dropped from under them; they had fallen into the *Marsh of Despondency*.

Instantly, they began thrashing, making things worse. Then, slowly, they were swallowed up in this unexpected *Despondency*. Finally, *Pliable* grabbed a branch near the edge and pulled himself out. While scraping the gooey mud from his clothing, *Pliable* unloaded. "I didn't sign up for this; you can have your *Way*. I'm going back! You're on your own, buddy; good luck, and enjoy your journey!

So, *Pliable* stormed off while Chris pleaded for *Help*. Chris slowly descended into *Despondency*; all the rejection, pain, and loneliness caught up with him. Finally, Chris cried out, "What have I done? Now I'm alone; I may die here if I don't get out." Then, up to his armpits in mud, Chris went quiet and hung his head, "I can't do this alone; I'm doomed."

With only a little daylight left, Chris heard a man singing.

The song became louder. Then appeared a large man; he stepped to the edge of the marsh then asked, "What happened?"

Chris, dripping with embarrassment said. "Well, I became exhausted and wasn't paying attention; I stepped right in."

With a laugh, the man extended his arm and pulled Chris out. Now relieved, Chris addressed this large happy man.

"Thanks, sir, thank you so much; if you hadn't shown up when you did, I would have perished!"

"No problem young man. What's your name."

"Chris, short for Christian, and yours?"

"*Help*, my name is *Help*, both first and last name."

"Chris responded, "Pardon me, but that's an unusual name."

"I suppose you're right, but I often hear *'Help'* from strangers seeking *The Way,* so I adopted the name."

Chris let out a laugh of his own, feeling much better.

Help gave Chris a bucket of clean water "Here, let's get you cleaned up, get food in your stomach, and some rest before tomorrow." Chris agreed and accepted *Help's* help.

Help remained with Chris while he prepared dinner and built a campfire. They sat near the fire, soaking up the waves of warmth flowing over their bodies. The night was clear, and the stars glimmered within the black expanse; this revealed to Chris the stupefying certainty of an *Almighty God*.

The evening noise enthralled Chris. The owls, insects, and the wind added to this unique moment. Then Chris probed *Help,* "Where do you live?"

Help, Helps Chris

Help answered. "In these parts close to the path. I roam around and *Help* those seeking *The Truth.*"

Chris became fascinated with this rare kind of man. "How long have you been helping people walk this path?"

Help grinned. "For eternity!"

Chris laughed. *Help* told Chris that, over time, He had rescued millions, including well-known people like Moses, King David, the Apostle Paul, and Mary Magdalene.

Chris was befuddled, wondering if *Help* was joking, so he changed the subject. Then, exhausted, Chris fell asleep. Throughout the night, he had dreams of his family, pleasant dreams.

At daybreak, Chris awakened from a deep sleep. While stretching, he looked around and discovered *Help* was gone. However, He left Chris with a few necessities for the trip;

food, fresh clothes, and new shoes. Then Chris saw a note: "Remain on this path; your next destination is *The Gate*."

Chris wondered, *will something good happen at this Gate?* Now alone, he began talking to himself. "Boy, if *Help* had not shown up, I would have been a goner. I'm beginning to believe now what the old biker said, God loves me and will provide. I can't explain this, but it happened!"

So, for the first time, Chris sat on a fallen tree, opened The Big Black Book, and began to read. *Goodness, there are some radical things in this Book; this will take time to assimilate.* Strangely, one passage jumped out. So, Chris read it aloud several times. "**We are no longer to be children, tossed here and there by waves and carried about by every wind of doctrine, by the trickery of men, by craftiness in deceitful scheming.**" Ephesians 4:14

Wow, this must be important! Now nervous, Chris gathered his things and headed up the trail cautiously. *Boy, it's a beautiful day; I wonder how long this will take; I want to get back to the family as soon as possible.*

Loneliness set in as Chris drudged on. Then he saw a smart-looking character coming toward him through the field. He caught up with Chris, then skipped a step to get in sync. "Hi there, the name is *Wiseman, Worldly Wiseman!* Where are you going so overloaded?"

"My name's Chris, sir, and a friend told me to head to *The Gate*. I'm supposed to receive instructions on how to get this load off my back."

"Who in the world told you that?" asked *Wiseman*.

"A friendly man named *Help* helped me along *The Way*."

"Well, what he told you is hogwash! I've been around a long time, and that advice gets you into more trouble, like that mud hole you slipped into! If you stay on that path, you'll suffer embarrassment, not to mention the pain, hunger, and poverty that awaits you. So, that Big Black Book, dump it!"

Worldly Wiseman narrowed his eyes. "Now look, Chris, you're too intelligent for that medieval nonsense; it's all a fantasy! Besides, why are you messing with things too deep for you?"

Wiseman continued to run his mouth, and Chris was all ears.

"Now, listen to me, Chris; I know how you can rid yourself of that burden you carry, and my way is painless."

"Well, tell me then, I'm tired of carrying this load," Chris replied.

"Good, now pay attention; over the next hill, there's a path off to the right, and at the end of this windy path is a village, the prettiest darn village you've ever seen. It's a really *decent* place with all kinds of *decent* people. And the mayor, he's a *decent* man. He has a *decent* son who is now his father's right-hand man. Are you still with me, Chris?"

"Yes, Sir, I'm paying attention!"

"Okay, now, the mayor's name is *Lee,* short for *Legality.* His son's name is *Civility.* And the name of this *decent* town is *Morality.* These *decent* people will help you with your load."

Chris's face brightened. "That sounds good to me; it sounds really *decent!* Excited now, Chris asked *Worldly Wiseman* to repeat the directions.

Not liking the interruption, *Wiseman* placed his hand on Chris's shoulder, then whispered. "Okay, son, I'll tell you one more time. Go right at the first path, over the hill. This will wind downward; the first house you come to is *Legality's;* stop there."

Chris adjusted his load, then thanked *Worldly Wiseman.*

Worldly Wiseman

"My pleasure," responded *Wiseman.* "Take care, and remember, get rid of that book!"

Chris plodded on and became lost in his thoughts." *Wiseman is a wise man; from his sharp appearance, he must be a professor of philosophy at an elite university. I'm sure glad I bumped into him!*

At last, he reached the path and changed direction. Chris remembered *Wiseman's* advice. He took his Big Black Book and hurled it into the field. "There, things should get better, and soon I can unload my burden." Unfortunately, it didn't take long before the bright green countryside became a dusty, pathetic brown. Next, the path became rocky with deep crevices. Chris struggled to remain on his feet. Then finally, hot, dry air gusts engulfed Chris in a whirlwind of dirt and tumbleweeds.

In the distance, a village appeared, floating in and out like a mirage. Chris located *Legality's* home per *Wiseman's* directions. He sensed that *Legality* lived a secluded secret existence because of the high walls, rod iron gate, and thick, overgrown vines surrounding his property.

I expected something different, thought Chris. Cautiously he approached the rusty gate where a sign read, "*Go Away.*" Chris spun around, "Wow, go away!? One thing for sure about *Legality;* he's not welcoming, and it appears he's hiding something. Now I'm beginning to think that *Legality* has no desire or ability to remove anyone's burden."

Chris's countenance rapidly changed, then he asked himself. *Is it possible Worldly Wiseman deceived me? Did the passage in The Book this morning warn me about Worldly Wiseman?"* Not yet ready to concede that good ole *Wiseman* was a wolf in sheep's clothing, he continued towards the village. Getting closer to town, the hot, dry air made Chris parched. *This is no place to have my thirst quenched,* Chris thought. *There should be some decent, moral folks who can help me.*

Further up, Chris discovered a ghost town, old wooden structures that had fallen apart; some burned to the ground. *This is the village called Morality? My goodness, there's not a soul here!* He walked a bit more, then Chris finally saw some people in front of a well-kept archaic church. However, his excitement dissipated when he saw them walking around in circles, slow and stiff, with the same weight of burdens on their backs. Notably, they looked unhappy, even though they

Wrong Way

religiously followed all the church's codes, tenants, rules, and laws.

I'm not stopping here; this looks like death! Curiosity pushed Chris on. *I must see where this path ends.* Chris heard groans and cries from the old buildings, making him tremble.

Then, the village was behind him at last, and the trail ended at the edge of a deep cliff. The sign at the end read *Dead End*.

Realizing that he was snookered, Chris became embarrassed and outraged. Not only was he angered with *Wiseman*, but himself, for being gullible and not heeding the clear warning from The Book. *Oh no, The Book! I must go back and find it!* Chris did an about-face and raced back through the village and the twisted path. Hours later, he arrived, panting, and dripping with sweat. In the tall grass, Chris began searching for The Book.

Where is it? This could take forever! Wait, what's this? Yes, I found it! While celebrating his find, his foot bumped into another Book, then another. *Oh no, there are thousands of*

Books here!

Chris fell to his knees, praying while looking for The Book. *Not all these books look the same; I must find the one with the gold inlay, Pastor Jimmy.*

While searching, Chris could not help wondering what happened to all the poor souls who never returned to retrieve their Books. *The cliff! They must have fallen over the cliff! Who was this character, Wiseman? Like a wolf in sheep's clothing, his impressive appearance persuaded me to believe he was intelligent, wise, and fatherly. So, I fell for it, hook, line, and sinker! I hope I never run into his kind again!*

At last, Chris found The Book and began leaping with joy. *I found it, I found it! I'll never let The Book from my sight again. This is my map, my guide; I must learn more!*

Now relieved, Chris walked to the edge of the field to recuperate. After he refreshed himself with water and food, he leaned against a tree and opened his *now* cherished Big Black Book.

Looking for further direction, he found a passage that read, **Enter by the Narrow Gate; for the Gate is wide, and the way is broad that leads to destruction, and many are those who enter by it. For the Gate is small, and the way is narrow that leads to life, and few are those who find it.**
Matthew 7:13

Chris spoke out loud. "That gives me goosebumps! This passage even called out my city, *Destruction!* So, I'm heading back to the straight and narrow path at the break of dawn."

Chris continued reading The Big Book, then fell asleep.

Chapter 4
The Gate

Rise and shine! Chris jumped up, eager to go. While walking back, he began a conversation with himself.

What was old Wiseman trying to convince me of? All this stuff about being decent, civil, and moral sounded good, but it's not how to get this load off my back. Shoot, I know many proper, polite, and honest people. They go to church every Sunday. Some volunteer to help the poor and homeless. This is admirable; however, they bear the same burden as me! It makes me wonder if they missed something fundamental.

Also, I've noticed that some become strict and judgmental, unable to enjoy life. Those who pride themselves on their high spiritual rank are the ones who derive enjoyment looking down their noses at others. Their load is just as heavy as mine, so old Wiseman lied to me! Indeed, we all should strive to become decent and moral people; however, if I thought I could unload this burden alone, I wouldn't be walking this path now. No! There's another Way, the only Way, and I will find it!

Back on the path and heading for *The Gate*, Chris was happy this episode was behind him. He arrived at *The Gate* a short time later. It was small and set into a massive high wall of chiseled stone blocks. Above *The Gate* read, KNOCK AND IT WILL BE OPENED. *Matthew 7:7*

Chris got the ominous feeling that he was being watched, so

he began banging on *The Gate*. "Let me in; please let me in!"

Then, finally, a voice was heard. "Who's there? Where did you come from? What do you want?"

"My name is Christian! I'm from *Destruction City* because that's where it was leading me. I'm desperate to find *The Truth.* The Big Book says this is the only entrance."

The Gate opened slowly, and an older man grabbed Chris and quickly pulled him inside, then slammed *The Gate* shut.

Bewildered, Chris asserted, "What's that all about?"

Goodwill secured *The Gate*, introduced himself, then answered. "There's opposition lurking out there, well-funded organized groups vehemently opposed to *The Way,* and anyone attempting to find it! They are spread throughout the world to hinder those seeking *The Truth.*

"These deceived people are pawns as they burn churches and destroy public displays that depict *The Almighty.* In addition, *The King's* servants are targeted with threats and intimidation. They aim to silence those who have pledged allegiance to *The King.*

"Even cowardly corporations and politicians aid these workers of iniquity, donating enormous amounts of money to their fraudulent organizations. They're afraid of being labeled intolerant by these evil activists. And behind all this wickedness are the invisible forces of darkness controlled by **the god of this world.**" *2 Corinthians 4:4*

Chris responded, "That's sobering, and I believe what you said is true. That's why I'm on this path. By the way, *Mr. Goodwill,* my name is Chris, sort for Christian, and I'm thrilled to be here. This is exactly where Pastor Jimmy, *Help,* and The Big Book said I should go."

Enter

Goodwill invited Chris into the dining room, where he served a hot meal and ice-cold lemonade. "So, tell me about your journey, Chris." Feeling rejuvenated, Chris recounted his encounters along the path to *Goodwill*. "*Obstinate*, that stubborn old kook, just blocked his ears; he tried so hard to prevent me from leaving. Finally, he ended his effort by calling me an idiot!

"Then there was *Pliable*, and *Pliable* was precisely that! At the first sign of trouble, he changed his mind and abandoned me in a mud hole. If not for *Help* showing up, I wouldn't be standing here now. Then *Worldly Wiseman*, that sly old snake, sent me down the wrong path. I lost a lot of time but learned some valuable lessons."

Goodwill answered. "Yes, many never made it past *Worldly Wiseman*." He's very good at beguiling people's minds. You're safe now, Chris, but you have a long way to go. Unfortunately, there will be many hazards to avoid before you arrive at your destination. However, *The Way* is simple."

Chris asked, "What do you mean?"

"Well, the path is both straight and narrow. So, if you get off onto a winding trail, you'll know you need to do an about-face and quickly get back."

Chris leaned back in the chair, satisfied with his meal, then asked more questions of *Goodwill*. "Tell me about this *Gate?*"

"Sure, Chris, millions have knocked on this *Old Gate*, and regardless of who they are or what they've done, they are allowed to enter. Then I ensure they're nourished, get a good night's sleep, and receive instructions to continue their journey."

"How long have you been minding this *Gate?*"

Goodwill smiled. "Forever!"

Chris thought *this was strange; there seemed to be a pattern forming here.* Then Chris asked, "*Mr. Goodwill,* when can I get this load off my back?"

"Soon, Chris, but you have one more crucial stop first. There, you will learn some essential lessons for your journey."

Feeling upbeat, Chris said, "Sounds good; I'm ready to get going. Thanks for everything, *Mr. Goodwill!*"

With a pat on the back, *Goodwill* replied. "My pleasure Chris; take care and remain alert."

Chris said, "Yes, I will, goodbye."

Now refreshed and full of anticipation, Chris moved on with his thoughts racing. *That Mr. Goodwill was sure a kind man. I wonder what's next? I've learned so much, and I've just started my journey.*

Chapter 5
The Old House

*A*fter a long day's walk, Chris stood before a large time-worn house, alone in the countryside. *This must be my next stop over; the one Goodwill told me about.*

Plush patterns of white and red flowers surrounded the old white Victorian house. An elderly woman tending the garden rose from her knees to greet the newcomer. "Hello there, young man, you must be Christian!"

"Yes, Chris for short, how did you know?" "Oh, *Goodwill* and I communicate often.

"Unsure how they did that, Chris asked, "What's your name?"

"I'm *Hospitality*. My husband and I manage this house, keeping it pristine for those traveling the path." She pointed to two chairs among the flowers. "Come, Chris, have a seat and rest."

Mrs. Hospitality had two glasses of fresh berry juice waiting on the small table between the chairs.

Chris began. "I understand that this *Old House* possesses valuable lessons, along with nourishment and rest."

Mrs. Hospitality replied. "This is true; illustrations for wisdom and understanding. They will protect you along *The Way*. For example, these flowers have two colors, red and white. The reds represent the blood shed by *The Holy One*, who died for us, so we could be set free and forgiven of our sins. The whites represent the cleansing that happens when

Hospitality in The Old House

one receives *The Free Gift.*"

Feeling eager, Chris said. "Wow, I can't wait to meet this *Holy One* you speak of!" Soon, Chris, soon. Let's go inside and meet *Mr. Hospitality;* he will show you around." They entered the house where awaited a thin gentleman with a long beard and a gentle smile.

"Hello there, Chris; welcome to *The Old House.* Sit down and enjoy supper with us." With Chris's stomach growling, he wasted no time saying, "Yes, thank you!"

After a delicious bowl of stew and warm fresh bread, they moved to the living room for conversation. First, Chris told of his journey, then revealed his homesickness, "I miss my family, but I can't return home with this burden."

Then, *Mrs. Hospitality* leaned forward in her rocking chair, "Chris, I have some good news."

All ears, Chris asked, "Yes, what is it?"

"Word trickled down that your lovely wife, Angela, bumped into Pastor Jimmy at the annual fall festival. She learned that it was he who spoke with you about *The Way*. It wasn't long before the Pastor convinced her to do the same. So, I'm happy to report that your wife began her journey and is seeking *The Truth*. Remember, Christian, everyone's path is different. Angela's growth in this *Walk* is not in sync with yours. Love and encourage her, and let *The Holy Spirit* teach and guide her, just like He's doing with you."

Hardly able to speak, Chris uttered, "Thank you!"

Mr. Hospitality rose from his chair. "Come, Chris, let's go upstairs; I'll show you around." While climbing the stairs, *Mr. Hospitality* prepared Chris. "In this portion of the *Old House* lives a very discerning man known for his insight and wisdom; he is *The Interpreter*. He's been here since the beginning."

"The beginning of what?" Chris questioned.

He replied, "Creation!"

Stunned again, Chris attempted to process *Mr. Hospitality's* answer. *I'm becoming convinced that those helping me on this journey are of a divine nature.*

They entered the door to the second floor, where *The Interpreter* waited. Chris felt a peaceful presence inside and out, then began to see things with intense clarity.

The Interpreter took the lead. They entered a room similar to a salon. The dirt, dust, and grime were noticeable. Unable to hold back, Chris blurted out, "This place is filthy, and it stinks!"

The Interpreter agreed, then signaled a man holding a straw broom to enter and begin sweeping. "Now, watch Chris."

Quickly, choking clouds of dust swirled around the room, inducing Chris into an episode of gagging and coughing.

The Interpreter then waved in a young woman who sprayed the air with water, causing the dust to settle on the floor. Then the room was easily swept clean.

Puzzled, Chris asked. "What are you trying to tell me?"

"Look," began *The Interpreter,* "You're here because you were fed up with all the doom that surrounded you in *Destruction City*. So, you started this journey to find the cause of all your troubles, right?"

"Well, yes." Chris conceded.

"So, what I'm showing you is this. Like this room, the world and its humans are contaminated, dirty, and messy. This shows how man's attempt to clean up their messes only worsens it. However, the cleansing began when the girl came in and sprayed the room with water. Chris, the girl represents the *Good News* inside that Big Black Book you carry."

"What exactly is this *Good News?*" Chris asked.

"The *Good News* is that, despite humans inability to clean up their mess and throw off their burden, God has provided a *Way. The Truth* and *The Way* will be revealed to you shortly."

The Interpreter led Chris into the next room. Inside were two young boys. The one in the center with all the toys piled around him was named, *Now.*

"As you can see, he's mean and selfish, coveting every toy in the room. If *Now* doesn't get what he wants, when he wants it, *Now* has a fit and begins to cry until he gets his way. Like those grown citizens in *Destruction City,* having more possessions and wanting them *Now* has become their obsession. They're ignorant to the eternal riches that could await them beyond their current world."

"What about the boy sitting in the corner?" asked Chris.

"As you can see, there are few toys near him. Instead, he sits in his chair with his eyes closed, with a peaceful glow on his face. He's focused on what awaits him beyond the present; his name is *Patience.*"

Closing the door, *The Interpreter* asked, "Isn't this one of the reasons for the troubles in the city you left?"

"Definitely," responded Chris.

"Christian, this is not a lesson of self-deprivation and making yourself poor. On the contrary, The Book clarifies, **Seek first The Kingdom of God, and His righteousness; all these things will be added to you.** Matthew 6:33 It's about the heart and priorities. But, The Big Book continues, **for where your treasure is, there will be your heart also.** Luke 12:34

"You see, Chris, man's heart is in a fallen condition, having an insatiable appetite for more. They believe more will bring happiness and fulfillment, but in the end, the emptiness is still there, void of satisfaction. The possessions and riches on this earth are for a fleeting time; however, the treasures in heaven are forever."

The Interpreter led Chris downstairs and out the back door to continue the lessons. Off in the trees stood a massive stone wall covered with green moss and vines. Looking north, a small man was throwing buckets of water on a fire at the base of the wall.

Chris thought *These illustrations were bizarre!*

"What's this supposed to reveal?" asked Chris.

Interpreter began, "The little man's name is *Frantic* because he's frantically trying to extinguish the fire. He's frustrated because it will not go out regardless of how much water he dumps on the fire. Now, let's go to the other side of the wall.

There, they found another man pouring oil into an opening to fuel the fire. Again, *The Interpreter* explained the meaning of this odd scene. "The man pouring the oil represents the invisible presence of *The Holy Spirit*. The oil that fuels the fire is the oil of gladness for those serving *The King*. Now the little man on the other side is the enemy of *The King*. His job is to extinguish the fire in every heart of those who belong to *The King*. The water symbolizes discouragement, guilt, embarrassment, and depression that plague *The King's* servants. However, when those loyal followers remain close to *The King*, the oil will continue to supply the flame in each believer's heart."

Chris was astonished! "This is quite an education!"

The Interpreter signaled. "Come, Chris, there's more."

As they ventured further into the woods, suddenly, a rock whizzed by Chris's face. "Stop here and take cover," ordered *The Interpreter*. Chris hid behind a tall redwood tree, then said. "This is dangerous. What's going on?"

The Interpreter answered. "Men hide behind trees engaged in rock fights. Each man represents a church. And each church was named based on a favorite doctrine for which they are passionate. Some believe you can only be saved if you agree with them. Sadly, they never understood the *Good News*.

"Christian, listen to this from The Big Book. **But I am afraid** that, as the serpent deceived Eve by his craftiness, your minds will be led astray from the simplicity and purity of devotion to Christ.** 2 Corinthians 11:3 The Big Book clearly defines the *Good News*, and these men have lost their way!"

The Interpreter pointed to another passage in The Big Book. **But if you bite and devour one another, take care that you are not consumed by one another.** Galatians 5:15

Chris questioned *Interpreter,* "Do all churches do this?"

"By no means, Chris! Many of *The King's anointed* leaders are faithful; they tend to His sheep, giving them guidance, correction, and love, and they serve with pure hearts, ensuring *The King* is honored and glorified.

"But, unfortunately, they are often attacked within and without because they do. *Our King* warned us in The Big Book of such matters. He comforts those who fall victim to these attacks. **Blessed are you when men hate you, ostracize you, and insult you, and scorn your name as evil, for the sake of the Son of Man. Be glad in that day and leap *for joy*, for behold, your reward is great in heaven."** Luke 6:21-23

As Chris and *The Interpreter* walked away, the sounds of men hurling insults and rocks at each other faded.

Further down, a crowd was gathered in front of a beautiful palace. Chris studied them, and what was evident was seen in their faces; they desired to enter the court. However, they were afraid. Guarding the entrance of the castle were several fierce-looking guards. Then, without warning, a short man broke through the crowd, outfitted with a helmet, breastplate, shield, and sword. Most notable was the expression on his face, pure unrestrained *Courage.* Suddenly, the little man bolted from the timid crowd and charged into the guards, leaving them spinning on the ground. Then, with a victory shout, he entered the palace.

By now, Chris knew what to expect from *The Interpreter*. So, he turned his head and waited for the interpretation. "Christian, this beautiful palace represents *The Kingdom of God* and *His Promises*. The little man's name is *Courage,* and he's doing just what The Big Black Book instructs us to do; **take The Kingdom by force.** Matthew 11;12 So, like a soldier who is utterly resolute in taking a city, So too is *Courage* unwavering in his pursuit to enter *The King's Kingdom.*

Chris said, "So, the rest in the crowd are paralyzed with fear, making them unable to experience the promises and blessings of *The King.*"

"Yes, Chris, you understand, and *Mr. Courage* will be dressed in the fine apparel of the palace and will enjoy an abundant life."

Chris nodded and said, "I'm starting to put this puzzle together."

Next, they came upon a dark, rundown house. Chris's first impression was neglect.

"You're right, Christian; this house has been neglected by its owner. Let's step inside." The door was opened, and right in the middle of the room sat the saddest, most defeated man Chris had ever laid eyes on. Wearing dirty ragged clothing, with a mop of tangled hair and an unshaven face, this poor soul looked at Chris with his head and shoulders sagging, in a posture of total *Helplessness.*

Chris cleared his throat. "How come you're in such a mess?"

The man lifted his head, "Oh, I got myself into this *Helpless* situation. The truth is I let myself wallow in self-pity while

Helpless

blaming others for my weaknesses. I've sat here so long that the floor has swallowed my feet."

"Chris asked, "How come you allowed this?"

"Well, I . . . I once was like you." The man leaned forward. "I was eager to discover *The Truth*; however, I was distracted and attracted to other self-serving interests. Then, before I knew it, I was pulled back into the harmful behavior I was trying to escape. I never did rid myself of the heavy burden

I carried. And, like many, I reverted to self-indulgent behavior. After a while, I couldn't care less about continuing my journey. Before I knew it, I was trapped in this prison of *Helplessness*. I never made it to my destination, where it's said people can be free. Unfortunately, I'm not sure anyone can help me now." *Helpless* continued bemoaning his past indiscretions and foolishness. "Oh, my name is *Helpless;* I'm sorry you had to meet me."

Then, Chris and *The Interpreter* left that very somber scene.

"That was extremely sad," Chris commented. "I must never allow that to sneak up on me!"

"You're right," answered *The Interpreter.* "This is why I have shown you these things. Bear them in mind as you continue your journey. May these warnings keep you safe along the way to *The Promised Land.*"

Chris looked up. "There are those words again, *The Promised Land!* That's it, *The Promised Land!* That's where I'm headed, and I'm on *The Way!*"

"Okay, Chris, that's all I have for you. I pray I've helped you and that you will successfully reach *The One* who will remove that heavy burden you carry. Goodbye, Chris."

"Goodbye, *Interpreter.* Thank you so much for revealing these important truths, I will guard them in my heart."

Chapter 6
The Burden Falls

Traveling on, Christian is full of anticipation and eager to discover what's ahead. *The Way became steep*, with tall stone walls bordering the path. Chris's mind wandered back to the lessons of the Old House. *How can this journey be completed with so many distractions and traps? It's as though invisible forces have colluded to prevent anyone from completing this journey.* Then came a passage from The Big Book. **Be on alert, stand firm, act like men, be strong.** 1 Corinthians 16:13

Christian was amazed this passage came to him so clearly. *Yes, that's exactly what I will do: be alert, strong, and act like a man!*

After several hours Christian stopped walking, *I'm hungry and thirsty, and this burden is unbearable*. With his emotions swirling, Chris became despondent as loneliness settled over him. He leaned against a tree weeping, then fell asleep.

His dreams returned him to times gone by, his childhood. Having been raised on a country farm, his fantasies placed him in a field of tall grass, running with his four-legged friend, "Skippy." Chris's mother's journey ended early, leaving his father to raise him and his older sister. So, much of his youth was spent with his grandmother. She was a sweet and sagacious woman. His mind swirled with thoughts of sitting alone with her, playing canasta, and eating ice cream. Sundays, Grandma walked Chris down the dirt road to the old schoolhouse for Sunday school. With Skippy waiting, Chris would finally exit the door, and off they ran to a large tree fort beyond the field, down near a creek.

These memories swirled around into pleasant dreams of a simpler time. Then, finally, Chris woke up feeling better and decided to move on.

The path continued up the steep hill, where an obstacle appeared. Moving closer, Chris saw an old wooden cross centered in *The Way*. Chris's heart leaped, then he ran to the foot of the cross. *This is it! This is where Pastor Jimmy and The Big Book told me to go! Here, the Lord Jesus Christ paid the penalty for my past, present, and future sins.*

Chris fell to his knees and embraced the cross. Then, with remorse and sorrow, Christian cried out, "Jesus, forgive me of my sins, and make me clean."

He remained on his knees, resting while reflecting. *So, this was the key!* **Godly sorrow brings repentance that leads to salvation and leaves no regret, but worldly sorrow brings death.** *2 Corinthians 7:10* Chris's *burden* dropped and rolled off into an empty grave. Christian celebrated, then proclaimed. "That's it, I found it! It's Jesus. **He's the Way, the Truth, and the Life!** *John 14:6* It is finished!"

Christian rose to his feet and stretched his arms, enjoying the feeling of freedom on his shoulders. "I'm free!" he shouted, "I'm free! The load is gone! His voice echoed over the vast canyon that sent flocks of birds to the sky. It was then the words of *The Savior* became a reality for Christian. **If the Son sets you free, you will be free indeed.** *John 8:36*

Then, when he saw the bloodstains on the old wooden cross, another reality sank in; the price that was paid for his

Free Indeed

freedom. Chris recalled passages from The Old Book; **Behold, the Lamb of God who takes away the sins of the world.** *John 1:29*

Realizing his allegiance was now with Jesus Christ, he whispered, "I'm a servant of Christ; I must follow Him and continue on this path."

A new outlook came over Chris. He no longer felt just a dirty part of a dirty scene. *I feel clean inside!* Enjoying his sense of freedom, Chris continued on the path with his mind racing; *indeed, there will be hardships ahead, and I know this will not be easy.* However, Chris now had a new attitude. And, with newness in life, strength, and purpose, he would face them all. Chris poured out his heart and thanked God for sending all those who helped him. He felt that he, too, wanted to be a part of bringing others to *The Truth.*

I might not be here today if it wasn't for Pastor Jimmy and others willing to reach out to strangers. Yes, I, too, want to get in on the action! No reward could be more significant than leading others to The Savior."

Then Chris recalled this from The Big Book. **For eye has not seen, and ear has not heard, nor has it entered the heart of man, what God has prepared for those who love Him.**
1 Corinthians 2:9

Chris pondered the significance of this promise. *That means no one can comprehend what HE has prepared for us. Indeed, it must be so powerful and magnificent that our human minds would explode! Splendor, love, and peace will permeate our new spiritual bodies. There will be no more lies, hate, cruelty, pain, sadness, guilt, and evil. This reality will be overwhelming! This is as far as my mind will take me, yet it's not far enough. One day, I will know.*

Chris snapped out of his thoughts and discovered two heavenly beings by his side. Unaware, he was now wearing a new set of clothes and had been given an identification mark. Chris looked back and saw his old rags lying on the path. Fearful he was naked, he quickly looked down and discovered he was clothed in a white robe. Euphoric, he began to dance.

"How did this happen?" Chris yelled.

One of the *Bright Ones* spoke. "Christian, although you were dead in your sins, you have been made alive with Him! You have been given this *Robe of Righteousness* because He is righteous. The Big Black Book explains. **I will rejoice greatly in the Lord, My soul will exult in my God; For He has clothed me with garments of salvation, He has wrapped me with a robe of righteousness."** *Isaiah 61:10*

Then, the other *Bright One* spoke. "Christian, everything has changed, you now have an inheritance that is **imperishable and undefiled and will not fade away, reserved in heaven for you.** *1 Peter 1:4* And, there's more! **Everyone who beholds the Son and believes in Him will have eternal life.** *John 6:40* Welcome to the family!"

The magnitude of this moment caused Chris to fall to his knees; he covered his face and wept. When he finished and stood, the bright ones were gone. Chris was stunned and overcome with astonishment and bliss.

The sun was setting, so Chris moved on and found a stream. He settled in between two boulders, opened the cloth bag his visitors left him, and pulled out food and a note; it read, **He must increase, but I must decrease.** *John 3:30*

Chris thought, *what a powerful pronouncement to the one who just committed their life to The Savior!* Nothing could be said beyond this; Chis now realized his mission and purpose. Feeling fulfilled, he walked to a stream and refreshed himself.

Not yet ready for sleep, he started a campfire to stay warm. Leaning back against a tree and staring into the fire, Chris reflected on the most important day of his life. He recalled the story where Jesus told Nicodemus; **unless one is born again, he cannot see The Kingdom of God – that which is born of the flesh is flesh, and that which is born of the spirit is spirit. Do not marvel that I said to you; you must be born again.** *John 3:3*

Deep in thought, Chris could not help but marvel. *So, this is precisely what happened when I said yes to Jesus; I was born again! Now I'm a child of The King, and I have inherited His kingdom! Today is the first day of the rest of my everlasting life.* Finally, he fell asleep.

The following morning, Christian was awakened by birds in the trees. He hurried to continue his journey, and jumped on the trail. Chris set a fast pace while singing a verse from The Big Book; **This is the day the Lord has made; I will rejoice and be glad in it.** Psalms 118:24

Questions swirled in his mind while treading forward on this warm summer day. *How will my Lord use me? Am I to change my occupation?* These and other uncertainties were put to rest when a voice whispered, **The mind of man plans his ways, but the Lord directs his steps – commit your works to the Lord, and your plans will be established.** Proverbs 16:9. With that, he took a deep breath and continued.

Soon, he approached three sleeping men on the side of the path. They all had iron bands around their ankles and were chained to the trees. Snore erupted spasmodically from these three "beauties," causing a moment of humor for Chris.

"Hey, you guys, wake up! What's the matter with you? There are places to go and things to do! So here, let me take off those irons."

"Don't you dare touch them, "yawned *Simple.*"

Then *Lethargy* chimed in. "That's right, Stand down buddy!"

If that wasn't enough clarification, the third sluggish man barked, "Look here stranger, my name is *Presumption.*" He cleared his throat, then continued. "You got a lot of nerve interrupting our sleep; go away!"

Chris responded. "Now listen guys, these are dangerous parts out here. Who knows, a hungry lion could attack you, or you could get beat up and robbed. You stick around here,

Three Sleepers

sleeping your life away; surely something terrible will befall all of you. You must remain alert and be on your toes."

Chris's well-said exhortation fell to the ground. The three sluggish men snored on. *I don't understand how they cannot see their danger.* Chris shrugged his shoulders and went on his way.

Chris sat on a fallen tree up the trail and opened The Big Book. The passage read, **So then, let us not sleep as others do, but let us be alert and sober – making the most of your time because the days are evil. Do not be foolish but understand what the will of the Lord is.** *Ephesians 5:16*

It's apparent those three fellows have no time for The Big Black Book, thought Chris. *What a shame. It's disappointing that they sleep when they could serve The Savior.* Chris walked on, knowing that everyone would give an account for the *gifts* and *time* given them.

So, Chris continued on *The Way,* still basking in the glow of his new life. Then, his path led him into a serene setting where a Pergola covered with vines stood among boulders and field grass. A short path joined the Pergola to a nearby pond, and tall birch trees surrounded this beautiful countryside.

Then Chris heard a shout coming from a man sitting inside the Pergola. "Young man, come over here!" Chris focused, then saw a rugged, robust man seated at a table. Chris walked over and introduced himself. "Hello, sir, I'm Christian; this is an awesome place you have!"

Wearing fatigues, a fur coat, and a beard, the man replied in a deep voice. "Hello there, Christian, welcome to *The King's* estate; my name is *Jon B*, please, sit and rest."

Jon B rose and stepped over to a well. He turned the wooden crank and pulled up a bucket of clear cold water. Then he returned and filled up a large goblet. Sitting on the table was a fresh loaf of bread. Chris looked at the bread and water, then raised his eyes.

Jon B sat down and then asked Chris, "Are you hungry? Chris nodded his head; *Yes.* Then again, he asked, "Are you thirsty?" Again, Chris answered, "Yes."

Okay, Christian, dig in until you're satisfied!"

Jon B offered Chris some honey for his bread, then opened his Big Black Book and read aloud. **"Then Jesus declared, I am the bread of life. Whoever comes to me will never go hungry, and whoever believes in me will never be thirsty.** *John 6:35* Son, do you understand what I just read?"

Chris answered, "I think I do; but please explain!"

"Chris, from now on, you need to look no further to fulfill your soul's thirst and hunger as long as you remain near

Him. **Come near to God and he will come near to you."**
James 4:8

Then *Jon B* invited Christian for a swim in the pond. Chris raised his arm and sniffed. Not pleased with the stench, he replied, "Yes, let's go!"

They got up, ran to the pond, and dove in. After they were exhausted, *Jon B* asked Christian, are you ready to be baptized?"

Chris replied, "I suppose so, but why?"

Jon B, seeming to have all the answers, explained. "Baptism is when you drive a stake in the ground for all to see, proclaiming that you now belong to *The Savior.* When you descend into the water signifies that the old Chris is dead. Then when you ascend, it means that you have repented your sins, and risen with Christ. The apostle Paul explained it. **We were therefore buried with him through baptism into death in order that, just as Christ was raised from the dead through the glory of the Father, we too may live a new life.** *Romans 6:4*

Christian is all in. "Let's do this!"

So, *Jon B* began. "In the name of *The Father, The Son,* and *The Holy Spirit,* I baptize you, Christian." Down into the water went Chris, and then up again. Chris took a deep breath, then exited the pond feeling renewed in body and spirit.

Nighttime arrived, so Chris accepted *Jon B's* invitation to join him for the evening meal and to spend the night. *Jon B* started a fire in a circular stone pit. The meal was peculiar, wild honey, carob beans, and fish. After several bites, Chris commented, "Not bad!"

The following day, Chris rose early to move on. After thanking *Jon B* for his hospitality, Chris asked. "By the way, what does the *"B"* stand for?"

Jon B answered, "Baptist."

Startled by his answer, Chris concluded that *The King* had directed his steps. Farewells were exchanged, then Christian departed from this unusual encounter.

It was not long before two sharp-looking characters caught up to Chris. His first impression was that these two men looked righteous! Winded, they proceeded to introduce themselves.

"Hello there, young man, my name is *Mr. Hypocrite,* and my good friend here is *Mr. Formalist.* And who do I have the pleasure of meeting?"

Thoroughly befuddled, Chris answered, "Hi, my name is Chris, short for Christian."

These two pious-looking gentlemen proclaimed they were headed to the same destination as Chris. So, Chris asked, "How did you get here? I haven't bumped into you throughout my entire journey!"

Simultaneously they piped up. "We just climbed the wall back there; there was no point walking that long rocky path you chose."

Chris, now concerned for these two polished-looking men, spoke up. "You know, according to The Big Book, you took a shortcut." Chris read to them, '**Truly I say to you, he who does not enter by the gate into the fold of the sheep but climb up some other way, he is a thief and a robber. I AM the Door; if anyone enters through Me, he shall be saved**. *John 10:1* Gentlemen, these are the words of Jesus Christ."

Hypocrite objected. "Now you listen, young man, whom do you think you are, telling us this ridiculous nonsense?"

Formalist & Hypocrite

Unbeknownst to Chris was that *Hypocrite* relished instructing others how to live their lives, giving him a feeling of superiority. He was judgmental and self-righteous; however, *Hypocrite* practiced the same sins in the darkness that he taught others not to do.

Now, Mr. Formalist measured his religiosity by outward appearance. Formalist appeared devout, attended church faithfully, and fervently practiced the sacraments.

Then *Formalist* jumped in, "Look here, son, you need to respect your elders and realize that we have much more wisdom than you."

Extremely agitated, *Hypocrite* took over, "Don't you think it's rather closed-minded believing there's only *One Way* to the *Promised Land?* We were raised in the church, and we both attend services religiously!"

Once again, *Formalist* jumped back in with a zinger. "Boy,

we're just as good as you! You don't fool us walking up this path with that Big Black Book. No doubt someone gave you that Big Book to make you look *righteous!*"

Chris shot back, "Yes, *Mr. Formalist,* what you said is true. *The One* who went before me, He died, that I might live, and the blood He shed made me clean.

So, yes, I am righteous, but only because He clothed me with His righteousness! Then He gave me the **sword of the spirit, which is the word of God** Ephesians 6:17 to guide and protect me. Never in a million years could I have earned *righteousness;* the cost is beyond anyone's ability. But, if you two had not jumped the wall, you would be clothed in *righteousness* also."

Stiff-necked and offended, *Formalist* snapped back. "Gibberish, boy! What's in that Book is way over your head and often misconstrued. You don't even *act* like someone who practices a church's *formalities* and *rituals.* So be on your way, Christian; you're still wet behind the ears!"

These two pompous geezers threw their chins up, did an about-face, then marched off, mumbling insults at Chris. *Hypocrite* took off to the left, and *Formalist* headed to the right. They shouted their last words at Chris, "We'll see you at the top!"

Christian would never see them again. *Mr. Formalist's* path led him into the tangled woods where wild beasts roamed. One pounced on *Formalist* and devoured him. *Hypocrite's* path led to a place with crevices and deep holes. While convincing himself that this was as good as any other way, he slipped and disappeared into the earth. What a gruesome end to these self-righteous individuals!

Chris pulled himself together. *Wow, Old Hypocrite and*

Formalist are sure they have this figured out. But unfortunately, they don't hold the words of Christ Jesus in high regard. Instead, they have made up their own rules about The Way and how to get into The Promised Land. I wonder if this is what The Big Book means when it says, **Do not give what is holy to the dogs and do not throw your pearls before swine, lest they trample them under their feet, and turn and tear you to pieces.** *Matthew 7:6*

Chapter 7
Strange Encounters

Chris dusted off his feet and continued on *The Way*. He stumbled up the hill and found a secluded place to rest. Exhausted from his last encounter, he feared more challenges to come. Chris opened fresh food from the bag that awaited him at the *Old Wooden Cross*. He leaned back to eat and then fell asleep. After his nap, Chris felt he had fallen behind, so he rose and began walking.

Then, two young men sprinted toward him at the top of a hill. Nearly knocking him to the ground, *Mistrust* and *Timid* came to a screeching halt. The dust settled while they attempted to catch their breath. Then, frightened, the two *Trembling Titans* began their rant.

Mistrust warned Chris, "Turn back quickly; you must turn back! Just down this hill are the two meanest dogs you've ever seen! They nearly ripped us to pieces; I almost passed out! Their growls were so vicious; we had no choice but to turn and run."

Timid cowered behind his friend. "You have no chance getting past those wild beasts!"

Chris asked, "Did your journey lead you to the cross?" Still shivering with fear, they both answered, "Yes."

"Well then, both of you are the heirs of *The King* and should rely on His edicts and promises written in The Big Book. Have you been learning about how *His Kingdom* operates?"

Timid & Mistrust

Timid and *Mistrust* hung their heads. "We took a nap where those three sleepers were, when we awakened, we rushed off, forgetting our Big Books."

Eager to set them straight, Chris told them, "You guys need to get back there as soon as possible and retrieve your Books. But then, study what's in The Book before you return."

Timid and *Mistrust* wasted no more time and began running. Now, after Chris's well-delivered exhortation, he felt good about himself. Then he looked down the path, and a wave of fear rushed over him. He realized he must heed his advice.

Before Chris continued, he sat to contemplate his next move.

Then, he opened his Big Book and searched. He found this comforting passage; **The Lord is my light and my salvation; Whom shall I fear? The Lord is the defense of my life; Whom shall I dread?** *Psalms 27:1*

Well, there's my answer, I must go forward, trusting Him for my safety. So, he rose and marched down the path.

Chris meditated on the promise repeatedly, attempting to keep his fear under control. Finally, he made it to the bottom, then reached into his pocket for The Book. "It's gone," he shouted. In panic mode, he wondered where it could be. "I can't possibly continue without it. Oh no! I left it back where I met up with *Timid* and *Mistrust!*"

Then the light went on. "I did exactly what *Timid* and *Mistrust* did; I left without my Big Book. I must go back and retrieve it!" Scurrying back, Chris beat himself up. "That's what I get for sleeping. This is terrible; what will I do if I can't find it!" Chris retraced his steps, feeling miserable. "I'll never get caught off guard like this again; I would have been gone by now without The Big Book!"

His many experiences convinced him that The Big Black Book is *The Word of God.* Several days earlier, Chris read that **All scripture is inspired by God and profitable for teaching, for reproof, for correction, for training in righteousness; that the man of God may be adequate, equipped for every good work.** *2 Timothy 3:16*

At last, Chris returned to the place where he rested. "There it is!" Now filled with joy, he breathed a sigh of relief. "Thank You, Lord!" He picked it up and secured it close to his heart, ensuring it was safe. Then, he returned to the path, lamenting the time lost due to backtracking.

He reached the spot where *Mistrust* and *Timid* high-tailed

A Test

back up the path. A terrible roar penetrated Chris's ears as he cautiously approached, sending chills down his spine. It was hard to breathe. Nevertheless, he inched forward until two big vicious dogs appeared.

Now, feeling empathy for *Mistrust* and *Timid,* Chris thought, *I see why they were so afraid; if those dogs get to me, they'll eat me for lunch!*

Amid all the confusion, Chris saw a man standing before a log cabin. Waving his hands, the man yelled, "Come, you have nothing to fear if you remain in the center of *The Way;* the dogs are chained."

Chris inched forward; then, both dogs vaulted at him. The hair on Chris's neck stood at attention to the snarling rage of these foam-flecked monsters. He moved forward cautiously and finally reached the man.

"Whew, that was scary!" Chris trembled as he approached. "What in the world are those beasts for?"

The *Caretaker* answered, "The *Master* of the house knows that those like yourself who seek *His Kingdom* will not find it without *faith* and *trust*. Just as it's written, **without faith it is impossible to please *Him*, for he who comes to God must believe that He is and *that* He is a rewarder of those who seek Him.** *Hebrews 11:6*

"Are you saying the dogs are there to test those of us on this journey?"

"Precisely," answered *Caretaker*. "It reveals the authenticity of an individual's trust in *The King of Kings.*"

Chris responded, "Well, it's effective!"

The *Caretaker* told Chris. "As you know, *Mistrust* and *Timid* were lacking. However, I got word that when they finally retrieved their Big Books, they talked, studied the scriptures, and prayed. They're headed back now, determined to get past these dogs."

"Well, that's good news!" said Chris. "I've read much about *The King's* mercy and grace."

"You're right, Christian; listen to this passage from The Big Book. **But God, being rich in mercy, because of His great love with which He loved us, even when we were dead in our transgressions, made us alive together with Christ; by grace, you have been saved.** *Ephesians 2:4*

"You see, Christian, we have a choice in every moment of our new lives. We can choose to *walk in the spirit* or *the flesh;* we can have the *mind of Christ* or the *mind of the flesh*. However, we suffer if we fail to put our faith in *The King* during seasons of fear. The apostle John made it clear. **There is no fear in love, but perfect love casts out fear because fear involves punishment, and the one who fears is not perfected in love.** *1 John 4:18* Christian, it's all about knowing how much The King loves us, and make no mistake; He love us!

"When *Mistrust* and *Timid* reach this porch, they will receive new identities, *Trustworthy* and *Valiant*."

"Wow! That gives me goosebumps," responded Chris.

Then, *The Caretaker* changed course. "Okay, let's get down to business. Step inside, Chris." He entered the cabin, and Chris followed, finding a cozy setting. In front of a stone fireplace were four lovely sisters. The fire crackled as it emitted warmth over Chris's chilled body. He took a seat facing the ladies, then *The Caretaker* spoke. "Chris, allow me to introduce *Prudence, Charity, Piety,* and *Discretion*."

Chris was astonished by the grace of these women. They were adorned with modesty and kindness, giving them divine beauty. They talked with him like a dear brother they hadn't seen for years. The young women asked Chris many questions about his life and family. Genuinely interested in his welfare and happiness, they shared valuable information about his future journey.

They appeared to be well acquainted with their *Master*. Chris hungered to learn more about Him and clung to every word the sisters spoke. He noted that the four young women mentioned this One they called *Lord* with such affection. So many names they used to describe Him: *Savior, Father, Master, King, Deliverer,* all spoken with reverence and gratitude.

There was a pause, and *The Caretaker* told Chris the sisters

FOUR GODLY SISTERS

would share their stories. Each one read a passage from The King's Book explaining the reason for their names. Then they prayed and began their testimonies.

Prudence started. "Dear brother, I was reckless and foolish before entering *The Kingdom*. My choices were always based on want, impulse, and vanity. This ruined my life, creating an unbearable burden. Then I came to the foot of the cross, the same as you and my three sisters. When I studied The Big Book, my mind was transformed. Now, I'm careful instead of reckless and foolish, having gained wisdom and understanding. I serve my *Lord* by imparting this to others on *The Way*."

Stupefied and all ears, Chris looked to *Charity*.

"Chris, I grew up selfish and judgmental. I looked at people with fierce eyes, never wanting to be kind. In time, I became alone and alienated from my family. This was an unbearable burden I could not escape; my life was spinning out of control. Then, one day I was at the park weeping when a stranger approached me on a motorcycle. He was a bit odd-looking, but gentle and kind. He called himself Pastor Jimmy, then asked if he could share some passages from his Big Book."

Chris said, "Yes, that was Pastor Jimmy; he showed up in my time of need and convinced me to begin my journey."

Charity nodded, then continued. "I was also persuaded; I yearned for the peace and confidence I saw in him. Once I said yes to the One who hung on that rugged cross, He began changing my weaknesses into strengths. I became liberated by showing love to people, even unlovable people. Instead of judging, I give them mercy. The Big Book says that **'mercy triumphs over judgment,'** *James 2:13*, and it's true. I have been liberated, so I pass that on to others who enter this house.

Feeling *The King's* presence, Chris turned his gaze to *Piety*.

"In my former life, I did not benefit my family and friends. No one could depend on me; I was unfaithful and not dedicated to anything or anyone. I had become a miserable, unfulfilled person. After coming to my *Savior*, I craved to become that new person with whom my *Savior* would be pleased. So, I committed to seeking the One who saved me. Now I'm fulfilled, which gives me peace and joy."

Chris spoke. "Your testimonies are powerful and make me yearn for what you have."

Lastly, *Discretion* took her turn. "In my youth, I was a big mouth. I believed expressing my opinion was my right and a sign of courage. I offended and hurt everyone, then blamed them for not agreeing; I had no friends. I was weighed down with guilt, pride, and depression. Then one day, I bumped into an old classmate back in *Destruction City;* his name was *Faithful."*

Excited, Chris spoke up. *"Faithful* and I are friends; I hope to catch up with him on *The Way.* Forgive me for interrupting; please, continue."

"Faithful pointed me in the right direction until I reached *The One* who was punished for my indiscretions. And like my sisters, my weaknesses became my strengths, all for the glory of our *King.* I, too, learned from The Big Book to guard my tongue. Now, I think before I speak. And when I speak, they are words that edify, encourage, and heal. *Our King* wrote, **Let your speech always be with grace, seasoned, as it were with salt, so that you may know how you should respond to each person.** *Colossians 3:6* **Let no unwholesome word proceed from your mouth, but only such a word as is good for edification according to the need of the moment, that it may give grace to those who hear.** *Colossians 4:6* So, Christian, I have a new purpose, and I love it!"

Peace permeated everyone in the house. A peace that the world could not comprehend. Sensing what everyone was experiencing, *Caretaker* quoted a relevant passage; **And do not get drunk with wine, for that is debauchery, but be filled with the Holy Spirit.** *Ephesians 5:18*

The Caretaker explained, "This is what is happening; we are all filled with *The Holy Spirit!"* Chris nodded in agreement.

Then the sisters showed Chris around the house. They took him into the library. He saw shelves of books that stretched into infinity in every direction. "What's all this?"

Prudence answered, "Each book is a detailed record of the

millions of believers throughout time. They tell of the incredible hardships of every warrior who pledged allegiance to *The King*. These inspired individuals accomplished amazing triumphs that honored the One who redeemed them, also known as *Almighty God."*

Chris became fascinated and wanted to remain in the library to read the marvelous accounts of those old heroes and their adventures. He was profoundly affected and was stirred to live for this same cause. Chris recalled from his Big Black Book the words the *Great Shepherd* spoke. **My sheep hear My voice, and I know them, and they follow Me.** John 10:27 That's precisely what I'm going to do. I'm going to listen to His voice, and I'm going to follow Him. This is my purpose; this is my mission!"

Charity smiled. "You grasp *The Truth* now." The other sisters agreed.

Then *Discretion* said, "Christian, your book is being written now and will appear on these shelves when you enter *The Promised Land."*

Chris received this with excitement; on the other hand, it dawned on him the sober reality that his life was being documented.

In harmony, all four sisters turned and walked toward another door. Chris followed them into the next room and began looking around. He realized this was an armory with a massive inventory. *Discretion* looked at Chris, "The time has come for you to change your wardrobe. What lies ahead is dangerous, and you will need protection."

Chris responded, "I was expecting this; I've read from The Big Book, **Therefore, take up the whole armor of God, that you may be able to resist in the evil day, and having**

done everything, to stand firm. Stand firm, therefore, having tightened your thighs with Truth, and having put on the breastplate of righteousness, and having covered your feet with the preparation of the Gospel of peace; in addition to all, taking up the shield of faith with which you will be able to extinguish all the flaming missiles of the evil one. And take the helmet of salvation, and the sword of the spirit, which is the word of God."
Ephesians 6:10-18

The sister's responded. "You're right, Chris." *Prudence, Charity, Piety,* and *Discretion* joined in, each selecting a piece of armor that fit perfectly. When finished, they all stepped back, leaving Chris bobbing around, struggling to keep his balance.

"This is heavy," exclaimed Chris. The sisters laughed, then *Discretion* assured him, "You'll adapt quickly, don't worry!"

The sisters left the room. Chris followed, swinging his new sword. They sat in the family room, where *The Caretaker* had prepared *bread* and *wine* for communion. They entered sacred silence, then searched their hearts. Each took the bread, representing Christ's body, scourged on our behalf, taking our punishment for the sin we have done. And then wine, which represented the blood of Christ, shed for those who confess Jesus as Lord, the blood that cleanses us from all sin.

The night drew near, so the young women filed into the kitchen. One hour passed, and they returned with a scrumptious meal. The room filled with the aroma of gourmet food. The snapping and popping in the fireplace from the next room set a comforting background for conversation and occasional laughter. Chris was encouraged and lifted. With dinner over, everyone helped clean up.

The Caretaker and sisters said goodnight, then went to bed. Chris sat comfortably in the chair facing the fire. Knowing this day was one to cherish, he thanked *The King* for the blessings, then expressed his desire to be a diligent servant for his *Redeemer*.

Everyone was up at the break of dawn. After breakfast, Chris put on his armor and rattled out to say his goodbyes. *Prudence* and *Charity* adjusted his breastplate, then walked him to the edge of the hill.

Piety handed him a basket of food, and then *Discretion* told Chris that his friend *Faithful* from *Destruction City* was just a short distance ahead. Several years older; *Faithful* spoke with Chris like Pastor Jimmy. However, Chris was not willing to receive it then.

Now, filled with excitement, he wanted to catch up with *Faithful* to discuss things of mutual interest. *The Caretaker* pulled Chris aside and put his hand on his shoulder. "Christian, not far from here, you will come to an orchard of fruit trees. There you will see many *wayfarers* eating fruit while resting in the shade. There are valuable lessons for you to absorb. The owner of the orchard is buried on that land; however, his daughter is there to share fascinating stories about her father. Take your time, and listen intently to her words."

"Yes, *Caretaker*, And thank you for all you have done for me."

Chris moved on, waving goodbye as he wobbled up the trail in his new outfit. Then, over rolling hills and grassy meadows, he arrived at a parkland called *Fruits of the Spirit*. A majestic stone wall surrounded this vibrant orchard. Just as *The Caretaker* described, people like himself stood under the trees talking while feasting on mouthwatering fruit.

Inside sat a woman under the most stunning plum tree Chris had ever seen. "Come on in; it looks like you need to rest."

"Chris happily responded, "Yes, I think I will; I'm trying to adjust to this new get-up. My name is Chris, short for Christian."

"Welcome, Chris, my name is *Fidelity*, and this orchard is the fruit of my father's life."

Chris leaned forward, "Please tell me about your father!" So, with a friendly smile, *Fidelity* began.

"My Dad was an orphan. Sadly, his mother died during childbirth, leaving his father alone and devastated. Unable to pull through this tragedy, he began drinking heavily; he lost his job and neglected my father. Then, the authorities took my father away, and shortly after, his father was killed in a bar fight. I never knew my grandparents.

"After that, my dad grew up in various foster homes, some good and some bad. As a young man, he had a unique sensitivity to those who suffered abandonment, rejection, fear, and loneliness. One day he walked through the countryside, trying to make sense of it all. He came upon an old church with an older couple sitting together outside; their names were *Comfort* and *Guidance.*

Surprised, Chris replied. "I've heard of them; they're friends of Pastor Jimmy. He told me I would come to know *Comfort* and *Guidance* on my journey."

Fidelity smiled. "*Comfort* and *Guidance* took my Dad in and cared for him. It was there my father came to know his *Heavenly Father.* Instead of becoming embittered and angry, he chose a different path. He knew that the sins of his father must be broken.

"*So,* he decided to focus on the needs of others, not by his words, but by his actions. He read to me often from his Big Black Book, passages like these. **Little children, let us not love with word or tongue, but in deed and truth.** *1 John 3:18* So, he held to that decree spoken by his *Heavenly Father* for the remainder of his life*.*"

Chris stood and reached for a plum that hung above his head, then paused and glanced at *Fidelity.*

"Go ahead, Chris, compliments of my father." He picked the fruit, sat down, then took a bite. With juice dripping down his chin, he remarked, "This is the best plum I've ever eaten!"

Fidelity agreed. "When he left *Comfort* and *Guidance*, my father was determined to support and encourage anyone in his path. That's why he planted this orchard, for those who suffered the same abandonment as he. Each tree represents the tangible fruit of my father's life, and although he's gone, his fruit is still bringing sweetness into the lives of others."

Fidelity rose and motioned Chris to follow her. They arrived at a tree, and *Fidelity* resumed her story. "Christian, this is an orchard of *Love*, and each tree is a tangible product of that *Love*. This tree is *Patience;* the next one is *Kindness.* Over here is *Gentleness,* and there is *Self-Control.* There are many more, and all these trees are the *fruit of the spirit,* the evidence of *Love.* My father planted and nurtured these trees until he went home. Even now, his love blesses those walking *The Way.*"

Chris was astonished, "your father was a great man!"

Fidelity added, "Yes, he was, but moreover, he was humble, a man of few words but many deeds."

Then, Chris asked. "What was his name?"

Fidelity looked into Christian's eyes and answered, *"Nobility, a name he earned through reverence to The King."*

Chris kissed the daughter's hand and thanked her, "This is a powerful story that will alter my walk with *The King* forever." He bowed his head and then returned to the path.

Chapter 8
A Confrontation

Making his way through the valley, Chris reflected on his recent events. Still stirring in him was *Fidelity's* story of her father, *Nobility*. Chris concluded that *Nobility* was genuine, not seeking recognition; instead, he loved people. *I must do the same! If not,* **I will become a noisy gong or a clanging cymbal**.
1 Corinthians 13:1

Throughout his journey, Chris encountered many people he knew back home. Some walked faster, while others slowed, becoming tired. But, most regrettable were those who gave up and chose to return to their former life's doubts, fears, deceit, greed, and addictions. Perhaps the most disturbing was the pretense. Pretending to be happy, pretending to be successful, pretending to be righteous, pretending to love.

I'm so grateful that I'm not a part of that anymore; so many attitudes and choices are determined by the fear of what other people think. So, I will only be concerned with what my Lord thinks about me.

Suddenly, Chris snapped from his thoughts, noticing an uproar from the valley below. Something was headed for him at an incredible speed, leaving dust, clouds, and waves of darkness in its wake. Getting closer, whirlwinds and flashes of fire covered the land. Christian entered into a state of terror. The only thing that brought him a measure of hope was his armor. He secured his shield with his left arm, then got a firm grip on the sword with his right hand. Taking a firm stance, he planted his feet securely in the soil. Then, still unable to make out what was headed toward him, a thought came; *RUN!* Then a second thought; *If I turn around, my back will be exposed!*

So, Chris quickly prepared himself for the impending doom. Initially, he frowned having to put on the ancient iron-ware, but now, although old-fashioned, he thought, *This is the best fitting suit I've ever worn.*

Suddenly, an upheaval of wickedness towered over Chris with a flash of fire and a gust of scorching wind. Rolling, sneering coils of smoky black clouds separated from a monstrous creature staring down at him with fire and hate-filled luminous eyes. It was none other than *Satan* himself!

Chris bent his head back and stared upward. Then, trembling, his face became white as the knuckles that gripped his sword. Chris thought: *This is not good!*

In a deep gravelly growl, *Satan* said, "I know you! You're a citizen of mine. I'm the prince of the land you fled; therefore, YOU are MY subject. Turn around NOW and return, or I will eliminate you right here!"

"I WAS a citizen of yours!" Chris shot back. Strangely, there was little reaction, so he continued. "I became your slave for years, but what did I earn? Listen here, *Mr. Fallen Angel*, working for you only earned me misery, pain, shame, and suffering!"

Surprisingly, *Satan* attempted to negotiate with Chris. "Well, so that's what it is." The *Devil* winked. "Wages! Hmm, if that concerns you, I'll make you a sweet deal. You turn around and go home, and I will make you rich upon your return. I have many positions to choose from. Would you like to be a banker? How about a politician? They make all kinds of money. Maybe we could find a gold mine together, or I could

Christian Stands Firm

send you to Hollywood to become a movie star."

Abruptly, time came to a screeching halt, and everything around Chris froze in place, including *Satan.* This gave Chris time to evaluate the situation. *Everything is happening fast, and why is he trying to make a deal? He could crush me in a heartbeat if he wanted.* Then a light came on! *Or just maybe he can't! Am I giving him more power over me than he truly has?* Then, Chris remembered a verse straight from his sword. **Greater is He who is in you than he who is in the world.** *1 John 4:4 Whoa! That's powerful!*

Just as suddenly as time stopped, it started again. Standing tall, Chris replied, "Look here, offer me what you will, but I'm NOT going back! I've committed my life to the One who proved His love by dying on the Cross for me. I didn't have to work for anything but say yes to God's gift. My life is abundant now following Him!"

"Silence Christian! I'll make you another deal. Make your own terms, and I will let you be. Just remain my subject and take it easy on this extreme trip you're on; I can go along with that! You can pretend you're on this *Walk*."

"Oh no, no way, you slimy overgrown snake. Nice try, but I've had my fill of your world and your deception. I'm going to follow my new *Master*. So, *Beelzebub*, crawl back in your pit; I quit! I don't like you; I don't like your country, and I don't want your wages! Get lost!"

Satan blew fire from every orifice in his body, then screamed, "I've had enough of your foolish gab; PREPARE TO DIE! I'm going to snatch your soul right now!"

With that, he lunged at Chris! It felt like a locomotive of filth hit him. He staggered back, but his *Shield of Faith* deflected the attack. Then came a mighty blow to his head, but it had no effect. Valiantly, Chris fought back while thanking God for the steel wrap surrounding his noodle. After a blow like that, it was strange how his thoughts remained so clear. This fight was not a game, someone may get hurt or die. Chris knew that without his sword, he'd be extinguished by now.

Unexpectedly, the sword flew from his hand, leaving him defenseless. *Satan* had him down with this advantage, standing on his chest, ready to finish him off. Chris's hand touched the sword, giving him a surge of strength and courage. He stretched and firmly grabbed the sword, then drove it into the evil Satanic manifestation. With a deafening screech of filthy blasphemy, the creature spun around, spread its enormous bat-like wings, and flew away, leaving a trail of gooey slime flowing from its body. It was the smell of death, rancid!

Chris slowly straightened up and brushed himself off. Then, completely exhausted, he lay down in a patch of grass under an umbrella tree. While he rested, it felt like healing was being applied by unseen hands. The soreness and wounds quickly healed. Next, he refreshed himself with the bread and wine given to him by *Sister Piety*. Leaning back, his mind swirled with a host of thoughts. *How is it that I was able to overcome that attack by such a powerful onslaught of evil? Everything I've read in The Book is genuine!*

Chris opened The Big Book and read. **I love you, O Lord, my strength. The Lord is my rock and my fortress and my deliverer, My God, my rock, in whom I take refuge, My shield and the horn of my salvation, my stronghold. I call upon the Lord, who is worthy to be praised, And I am saved from my enemies.** Psalm 18:2 *Yes, this is how I feel; this I know is true; thank you, Lord!*

Finally, Chris fell asleep, confident that his *King* was watching over him.

A new day began, and Chris jumped up with enthusiasm. *Ahh, what a beautiful day; I wonder what's in store!* But unfortunately, the path descended further down from where Chris waged his battle with the *Downstairs Big Man*. Chris felt this wouldn't be the last time he'd deal with *Mr. Evil*.

He ate breakfast, packed up, then cautiously plodded down the path with his sword drawn. The angle was so steep that he struggled to remain on his feet. At last, Chris reached a point in the canyon where it was hard to see, and the games began.

Two men raced towards him around a bend, panting. Then, finally, one shouted. "Turn back!"

Not again! Thought Chris.

Self-love & Critic

"You must go back; you'll never make it!" cried the other man. Before they explained further, the first man told Chris their names. "I'm *Critic,* and this is my brother, *Self-Love.*"

Although *Critic* and *Self-Love* came to the path through the Cross, they spent valuable time on their journeys doing what they did best. *Critic* derived a sense of superiority and satisfaction when pointing out the flaws of others while being oblivious to his own.

His brother *Self–Love* wasted his time daydreaming of accomplishments as he imagined the admiration of others. Neither of them took the time to study the ways of their *King* recorded in The Big Book. Sadly, these brothers were ineffective in their *Lord's Kingdom;* as such, they inflicted hurt and anger upon their fellow brothers and sisters, creating more harm than good.

Critic and *Self-Love* told Chris, "Down in that valley is the shadow of death; it's cold and scary! There are traps, wild beasts, and muggers lying in wait; don't try it; you'll never make it!"

Chris decided they weren't prepared for whatever these two ran into down there. He questioned them. "Where's your armor? Didn't you stay at *The Caretaker's* House?"

Critic answered, "Once we got past the dogs, we hightailed it from the house where an eccentric man was waving at us, trying to get us to stop."

"That explains a lot," Chris replied. "I suggest you go back and visit *The Caretaker* and *The Four Sisters*. *Our King* put that house on *The Way* intentionally for our benefit."

Suddenly, a deep rumble from the valley shook the ground. Instead of responding to Chris, *Critic* and *Self-Love* turned and ran, leaving Chris to face the valley alone. Dread engulfed Chris. He thought, *how many times do I need to encounter these tests? This is not fun!* Now, filled with anxiety, Chris inched slowly into the cold darkness. The path narrowed and was becoming dangerous. He could barely see and was shivering. He made out one side: a deep ditch with ragged steep banks. A muddle of stink, mud, and slime was on the other edge. Smoke belched from the chasms below.

Hearing voices, Chris dropped to his knees and gazed down. He could vaguely make out a line of people following a *blind guide*. Then, with a surge of arrogance, the *blind man* loudly declared himself their anointed leader.

Chris saw the danger they were headed toward and shouted directions. A stern voice echoed back up the canyon. "Look, Mister, this is my flock, and I'm their Prophet! I know the way, so go about your business, or consider joining my sheep in our quest to paradise."

Chris shook his head and yelled back, "No thanks!" Then he heard screams from the canyon; the cries weakened until there were no more. Chris sighed. There was only one conclusion; their magnificent leader walked them off a cliff.

Chris recalled warnings from The Big Book that described this ghastly scene.

Let them alone; they are blind guides of the blind. And if a blind man guides a blind man, both will fall into a pit.
Matthew 15:14

Chris spoke out, "This is sobering; I must stay alert, for many are deceived, having believed the lies of blind guides, who masquerade as prophets and teachers of *The King*." He carefully crept forward; it took all his concentration to stay on this rough path. Occasionally, he heard cries or caught a glimpse of someone falling into the sludge. The bottomless hole was dragging down its victims. This was anything but pleasant, causing Chris to feel sick.

He struggled to continue navigating the tightrope of a path. He nearly lost his balance. Then, flying things began slapping at Chris; he heard screeching and whispering. There was the stench of pungent smoke; he could no longer think, only pray. Chris believed *Satan* had sent a legion of demons to harass him. One whispered foul things against God. The demon persisted, and Chris began to believe the thoughts were a product of his mind, making him feel like he'd committed a sin that could never be pardoned.

Dizzy and ready to vomit, Chris lay on the path. *This is too much to deal with in such a short time. I'm supposed to be strong, but how much can one take? I'm alone! I've never felt this close to death; I can't go any further.*

Christian curled up, then entered into the deepest sleep of his life. He dreamt of a bright angelic host coming from the heavens and settling over him, bringing warmth and comfort. Then, vivid images of King David entered his dream.

David, one of the most remarkable men ever blessed by *The Lord*, also traveled this valley. And, like Chris, David too sank into utter despair. But for the grace of God, he would have been completely lost.

Instead, as though sent back in time, Chris watched David writhing in anguish and remorse on the path. Weeping, David prayed. **Hide Your face from my sins And blot out all my iniquities. Create in me a clean heart, O God, and renew a steadfast spirit within me. Do not cast me away from Your presence, and do not take Your Holy Spirit from me.** *Psalms 51: 9-11*

Swiftly, David rose, took hold of his sword, then, with the roar of a lion, declared, **Though I walk through the valley of death, I will fear no evil!** *Psalms 23:4*

Chris awakened, jumped to his feet, sword in hand, and repeated the words of King David. Then, with a surge of courage and resolve, Chris shouted, "I've had enough of this; I'm climbing out of the valley!" Before his next breath, Chris found himself standing on a mountaintop. The view was clear, bright, and beautiful. He brushed away the ash, drank water, and lay beside the stream.

After Chris acclimated to the sudden change, he sat down, leaned against a tree, and stretched his legs. Chris threw a question into the wind, trying to make sense of it all. "Why must I suffer? I don't get it! I've had more tribulation as a child of *The King* than before!

Then a rustling of the bushes came from behind. Chris

cautiously separated the branches and peered through. There sat a young woman in a wheelchair without legs, and on her lap was a Big Black Book. She was snacking on grapes while reading, and her countenance glowed.

Chris stepped through the shrubbery to introduce himself. "Hello there, you surprised me; I didn't know you were here. Chris extended his hand. "My name is Chris, short for Christian."

"Hello, Chris; my name is *Tenacity*. I couldn't help but hear the questions you cried out, what's troubling you!"

Embarrassed and feeling small, Chris lowered his head and squeaked his answer.

"Well, it's just that I've had so many horrible things happen recently, and being a child of *The Highest*, I cannot figure it out! And now I see you in this wheelchair; I feel ashamed and don't understand how you are so poised considering your circumstances."

Tenacity responded. "Christian, make no mistake, I too struggled with the same questions, and I became angry with *The Highest,* even questioning *His* love for me. However, when I understood *His Ways,* I entered the peace and joy He intended for me.

Chris is intrigued by *Tenacity's* tenacity, then he asks. "How did you reach this level of tolerance and acceptance?"

"It wasn't easy, Chris; however, I was relentless. I had to put suffering and hardship in their proper perspective. So, I spent endless hours searching The Big Black Book. Would you like me to share with you what I discovered?"

Chris eagerly responded, "Yes!"

"You see, Chris, I've learned that our *Lord's* priority is for us to conform to *His Son's* likeness. Listen to this passage. **For those God foreknew he also predestined to be conformed to the image of his Son.** *Our Savior* spoke these words. **He causes his sun to rise on the evil and the good, and sends rain on the righteous and the unrighteous.** Matthew 5:45 And, **In this world you will have trouble. But take heart! I have overcome the world."** John 16:33

Chris reacted, "*Lovely,* so trials, and tribulations are part of our *Walk* until we reach the *Promised Land?*"

Tenacity laughed. "Yes, Chris, trials and tribulations can sometimes produce a good outcome. However, our response will always determine that outcome. So, Christian, please read this. *Tenacity* handed her Big Book to Christian, then he read aloud. "**But we also glory in our sufferings, because we know that suffering produces perseverance; perseverance, character; and character, hope. And hope does not put us to shame, because God's love has been poured out into our hearts through the Holy Spirit, who has been given to us."** Romans 5:3-5

Chris raised his eyes and said. "I understand now." Then he returned The Big Book.

Tenacity warned Christian, "Make sure that whatever suffering you endure is not the result of sin. Listen to this passage. **If you suffer, it should not be as a murderer or thief or any other kind of criminal, or even as a meddler. However, if you suffer as a Christian, do not be ashamed, but praise God that you bear that name."** 1 Peter 4:15-16

Tenacity asked Christian, "What do you think now?"

Christian answered *Tenacity* as a student would his teacher. "I've entered into a deeper understanding concerning my relationship with our *Heavenly Father*.

Then Chris asked, "Are you safe here alone?"

"Yes, Christian, I'm safe and well cared for! My husband returns here each day to take me home after I've spent time with *The King*. His name is *Michael;* he protects me; he's an *Angel*."

This encounter confounded Chris. He told *Tenacity* it was a pleasure to meet her and thanked her for sharing her wisdom. Chris walked back to the path and continued.

Chapter 9
An Old Friend

*F*eeling encouraged, Chris had a new surge of energy to carry him forward. In the distance, he heard whistling. Looking intently, he spotted movement ahead. *Could this be my old friend Faithful?* He picked up the pace, then yelled, *Faithful,* is that you?"

The man turned around and shouted back, "Chris, Yes, it's me!" Filled with enthusiasm, they began walking toward each other. They met halfway and embraced. "Boy, it's great to see you, Chris!"

"Same here, *Faithful!* You wouldn't believe what I've been through; it's been rough!"

Faithful replied, "Yes, I think I can!"

Now walking the path together, Chris's feeling of loneliness dissipated. *Faithful* slapped Chris on the back, "I can't express how happy I am that you decided to follow *Our Shepherd.*"

Chris replied. "Yes, *Faithful,* I remember you sharing *The Savior* with me. However, I didn't surrender because of my pride and fear of rejection. I recall the words of Jesus Christ you frequently read me from your Big Black Book. **I am the door; if anyone enters through Me, he will be saved, and will go in and out and find pasture.** *John 10:9* You knew I longed for fulfillment and purpose, and you were *Faithful* in showing me *The Way.* Thank you!"

But then, Pastor Jimmy came to me when I reached my

Faithful

end. "That's right, Chris; just like the words of our *Lord*, **One sows, and another reaps, I sent you to reap that for which you have not labored; others have labored, and you have entered into their labor."** *John 4:37* So, you see, Chris, *The Lord* puts those willing servants in our path to accomplish His purposes."

Chris agreed. "Yes, I see that now."

The two friends continued down the path, fulfilling what The Big Book described: **Iron sharpens iron, So one man sharpens another.** *Proverbs 27:17*

Faithful was in *Destruction City* when *Pliable* returned. He told Chris how *Pliable b*ecame indignant and self-righteous, denouncing Chris to the neighbors. "It was strange how they all despised *Pliable* for turning back, especially because of a little dirt on his pants."

Chris reacted with regret. "Boy, no mercy, I actually felt sorry for *Pliable!*"

Faithful agreed. "What is also sad is that they too need mercy; however, they haven't a clue." *Faithful* explained, "Many have searched for *The Truth* and began on *The Way;* however, they returned when trials or temptation caused them to stumble. Like The Big Book says, **As a dog that returns to its vomit is a fool who repeats his foolishness.** *Proverbs 26:11* Therefore, we must pray for them."

Faithful shared that he was at the festival when Pastor Jimmy spoke with Angela. "She broke down and became sorrowful for mocking and scorning you for pursuing *The Way.* They talked for hours, and near the end of their conversation, Angela said, 'I'm going to begin this journey; I'm going to join my husband!'"

"Yes, *Faithful,* this is true, *Mrs. Hospitality* told me. So now, the love of my life and I are serving our *Lord* in different ways, having different *gifts* given to us by Him."

Faithful shared with Chris the many encounters he'd had on *The Way.* The most frightening was with a married woman named, *Wantona!* While liberally displaying her voluptuous feminine features, *Faithful* mistakenly looked into her erotic eyes while she was telling him how much she admired him. She spoke about love, pure love, and original love. While the oil of her tongue seduced *Faithful,* she gave him the benefit of calculated views of her lovely body. Then, *Wantona* came in for the kill when she suggested, "Come aside with me for a little while; I promise you a delightful and delicious time!"

Faithful told Chris, "I was almost hooked and reeled in when the warning came from The Big Book out of the blue." **For the lips of an adulteress drip honey, and smoother than oil is her speech. But in the end, she is bitter as wormwood. Her feet go down to death. She does not ponder the path of life; her ways are unstable; she does not know it. Keep your way far from her, and do not go near the door of her house.** *Proverbs 5:3*

"I tell you, Chris, if those divine words had not been written on my heart, I surely would have surrendered to her powerful temptation. Then from within came a thought; *no one will ever know!* So, I spoke to that lie, *I will know, and so will the Holy One who died in my place to cleanse me of such sins.* Then more of our *Lord's* warnings flooded my mind. **Do not desire her beauty in your heart, Nor let her capture you with her eyelids. For on account of a harlot, one is reduced to a loaf of bread, And an adulteress hunts for the precious life. Can a man take fire in his bosom and his clothes not be burned?** *Proverbs 6: 25-27* "With that, I jumped back, turned around, and ran away. All the while, I heard this lovely creature screaming vulgarities at me.

Chris's eyes and mouth were wide open. "That was a close one!

"Yes, it was Chris. Fortunately, I did what our Lord instructed. **Your Word I have hidden in my heart that I might not sin against You.** *Psalms 119:11* "Admittedly, my thoughts are not entirely rid of her. I wish I'd never seen her!"

Faithful continued with another story of a character who tempted him. "His name was *Adam*, and he had complete control of a town called *Deceit*. *Adam* had a beautiful daughter. Whatever she wanted, he gave it to her."

Faithful paused for a drink of water, then continued. "*Adam* favored me, then asked, 'I have a proposition. As you can see, I'm a very wealthy man; however, I'm old. Come live with me; then, everything I have will be yours when I die. And, you can have my daughter and all my servants. Now look, this adventure you're on is silly. You can walk away from this path that forces you into a life of hard work and self-denial. End this now, come live with me, then you can finance others on this journey, making you good! In the meantime, you'll have your own promised land right here, right now! Why waste your life pursuing a pie-in-the-sky?'"

Chris reacted, "Oh wow, what an offer! You would never have worked another day in your life. So, what did you do?"

"I nearly caved! After all, *Adam* was sincere and seemed harmless. But then I recalled these same kinds of people back in *Destruction City*. They weren't happy, and all the riches, possessions, and idle time they accumulated eventually became a source of problems and stress.

"Then, sensing my caution, *Adam* began pleading with me, saying this was where I belonged. I needed to get out of there, so I told *Adam* thanks, but no thanks, then I left. He became angry and called me a fool.

"You see, Christian, with all these temptations since we've been on this journey, it's obvious that there's a concerted invisible effort to keep us from finishing our *Walk*. So, like you, brother, I'm more determined than ever. We will finish the course!"

Chris responded, "I'm with you *Faithful,* we must finish!" Chris was enthralled with *Faithful's* stories and asked for more.

"Okay, Chris, one more, then we need to get going. Back in *Destruction City,* I was hiking through the woods, then suddenly, from behind a tree, a man stepped onto my path and started walking next to me. He was a pious-looking fellow who lived in an ivory tower. He had no *Shame* telling me his name. 'Hello there brother, I'm *Shame,* Mr. Shame.' The first words from his mouth were that I was an embarrassment to him. He unloaded on me, saying pursuing this path was shocking, pitiful, and ignorant. He continued, 'You really believe you're following this invisible *Master* to which you have surrendered your life? Furthermore, watching you influence others to join you in this fantasy is embarrassing. Look at the record; how many wise men and intellectuals would consider such nonsense? This journey you are on is for the uneducated and the poor.'"

Chris interjected. "Wow, this guy was attempting to take you out!"

"Yes, he was," *Faithful* agreed. "Then he said it was embarrassing how we believers make a spectacle of ourselves with ridiculous public displays."

"What did he mean by that?" Chris asked.

"Praying in public upset *Shame.* And our efforts to publicly protect the unborn were an absolute embarrassment to him. So, I told *Shame* that he does the same for the Kangaroo Rat. Although that infuriated him, he persisted. I tell you, Chris, I had the hardest time shaking him; he followed me for miles, whispering negative suggestions constantly. Finally, I had

Mr. Shame

enough, so I called him a spineless hypocrite, and his *Shame* was a waste of my time. With that, he became offended and walked away. I was glad to see him go!"

"No kidding," Chris remarked.

Faithful continued. "After *Shame* disappeared over the hill, I needed to sit down to mend my mind. So, I opened my Big Book, and this passage awaited me. "**For I am not ashamed of the gospel, for it is the power of God for salvation to everyone who believes.**" *Romans 1:16* And then, the words of *The Savior* came to mind, **"Therefore everyone who confesses Me before men, I will also confess him before My Father who is in heaven. But whoever denies Me before men, I will also deny him before My Father who is in heaven.** *Matthew 10: 32-33* Chris, these were the very words I needed to hear from our *King*. You know, there was a time I thought moments like this were just a coincidence. But I don't think that anymore. Now, I am assured that it's *The Holy Spirit.* Our *King* promised to send *The Comforter* to guide, help, teach, and correct those who love Him."

Fixated and ready to respond, Chris told *Faithful* that he, too, had these moments, and they were magnificent.

Chris and *Faithful* trudged along, enjoying the quiet presence of each other's company, each lost in his own thoughts. Suddenly, a tall, thin man hopped onto the path interrupting their tranquility. He sported a toothy smile from ear to ear, then extended his hand. He proceeded to join them and quickly engaged them in conversation.

"Gentlemen, *Gab's* the name, rap is my game."

With no pause for Chris or *Faithful* to introduce themselves, *Gab* revved up his tongue. "I've been looking for someone to talk with; I love having discussions about anything! This is one of the joys of life, so what should we talk about? Something spiritual? I love conversing about spiritual topics. How about Eastern religion, metaphysics, or philosophy?"

Gab considered himself an expert on all topics and was ready to generously share his knowledge with anyone. "Politics, human behavior, or the Bible? Yes, that's it; I love The Big Book and the other books about God!"

Gab released a locomotive of verbiage on *Faithful* and Chris. Unable to get a word in edge-wise, *Gab* delighted only in expressing his thoughts, revealing the self-aggrandizing nature of this narcissist. *Gab* loved listening to himself while being void of interest in the opinion of another. The avalanche of verbiage continued to pour from *Gab's* mouth in a stream of never-ending wordage that nearly put *Faithful* and Chris into a coma.

Gab the Name ~ Rap's My Game

Faithful made several futile attempts to enter the conversation. He wanted to explain to *Gab* that the *Good News* was not only words but action. However, *Gab* rudely cut him off, injecting his interpretations and opinions.

Chris and *Faithful* finally gave up and went silent. It was hopeless and a waste of time trying to share a thought with this *Niagara of Yak*.

Once *Gab* had wholly exhausted himself, he openly concluded that his two companions were dull and boring. *Gab* told them they did not enjoy the same level of brilliance and intelligence as he. With that said, he created a lame excuse and hurried away.

Overcome by the sudden silence, Chris and *Faithful* looked at each other, then shook their heads in unison. They continued walking, enjoying the quiet.

Then finally, Chris spoke. "You know, I've read a lot about *Gab* in *The Big Book*. **Do you see a man who is hasty with his words? There is more hope for a fool than for him.**

Proverbs 29:20 **But let everyone be quick to hear, slow to speak, and slow to anger.** *James 1:19* **If anyone thinks himself to be religious and yet does not control his tongue but deceives his own heart, this man's religion is worthless.** *James 1:26*

Faithful commented, "Those are potent warnings from our *Heavenly Father*. But, unfortunately, *Gab* doesn't know as much as he thinks about The Book."

Chris chimed in. "There's so much wisdom in our Big Books, and it has a lot to say about our tongues. The tongue is depicted as **unruly and impossible to tame.** *James 3:8*

"That's not all," *Faithful added.* **The tongue is a restless evil, full of deadly poison!** *James 3:8* Our *Book* says, **with it, we bless our Lord and Father; and with it, we curse men; who have been made in the likeness of God; from the same mouth come both blessing and cursing. My brothers, these things ought not to be this way."** *James 3:9*

Chris agreed and continued to drive the point home with this potent visual. **Does a fountain send out fresh and bitter water from the same opening? Can a fig tree, my brothers, produce olives, or a vine produce figs? Neither can saltwater produce fresh.** *James 3:11*

They continued their journeys while soul-searching, occasionally mentioning verbal blunders that were destructive and hurtful. After several minutes of reflection, sorrow weighed heavy on their hearts for things spoken in the past, so Chris and *Faithful* stopped to rest and talk about it all. Chris confessed to *Faithful* that he was rebellious and disrespectful to his father in his teen years.

"My dad tried to warn me about experimenting with drugs, booze, and following the crowd. I answered harshly, telling him to mind his own business. I never apologized for that disrespectful statement, and now my father has passed, and I feel terrible!"

Faithful replied, "I know, even though it was in the past, it's like a nail in a door; you can remove the nail, but it leaves a hole. "Shortly after coming to our *Savior,* I got carried away and thought I knew everything. One day, I condemned my sister. I alleged her kids were spoiled and her husband was doing things behind her back. Mistakenly, I believed I was given spiritual discernment, but instead, I was self-righteous and judgmental. My accusation created a ton of hurt and division as wide as a canyon. So, instead of **acting like a man,** I pretended it never happened. *1 Corinthians 16:13*

"Then, when reading The Big Book, a passage hit me right between the eyes! **For God did not send the Son into the world to judge the world, but that the world might be saved through Him.** *John 3:17*

"I was awakened, or rather, slapped in the face! So, I asked myself, *if my sinless Redeemer did not come to judge; yet I, a redeemed sinner, do judge, then what had I become?* The answer shook me to the core. I had become a hypocrite, a religious Pharisee! This realization made me sick to my stomach!"

Astonished with *Faithful's* honesty, Chris asked. "Then what happened?"

Faithful jumped back in, "I wasted no time; I went to my sister and her husband and asked for forgiveness. That experience taught me a valuable lesson about my tongue and heart."

Thanks to their brush up with *Yakety-Yak,* Christian and

Faithful understood just how spot-on *The King's* proclamations are in The Big Book. **And the tongue is a fire, the very world of iniquity; and sets on fire the course of our lives and is set on fire by hell.** *James 3:6*

Finally, Chris and *Faithfu*l pledged to control their tongues.

Chapter 10
Deep Discoveries

"Wow, that's a strange site!" Chris exclaimed. They came upon two plots of land, one on each side of *The Way*. Both had a complex atop their hill, and a pathway that began several feet from *The Way*. Each path led up a hill ending at the door of two huge structures. These buildings belonged to religious organizations that asserted their way is *The Way*. However, their paths went in different directions, ending in *The Ditches of Deception*.

Christian and *Faithful* observed two well-groomed young fellows on the left wearing white shirts and ties. Smiling, they straddled their bikes while offering help to those on their journey. However, as respectable and kind as they appeared, their real motive was to convince those on *The Way* to change course.

On the opposite side was a proper-looking couple; they, too, studied a big book; however, it had been altered by those living in the tall tower atop the hill. They changed the *Good News's* fundamental truths, creating a religion of fear, deception, control, and bondage. Nevertheless, they presented themselves with a heavy dose of confidence as they offered their publications to those walking by. They were well-trained to twist and turn, convincing some to leave *The Way* and enter their kingdom. They sincerely believed what they publicized to those who entered the gate because they had been cleverly deceived. Numerous gullible followers of *The King* had been beguiled by their skillful manipulation of various passages.

These estates were surrounded by invisible barbed wire, creating mental and emotional barriers. The fence was built using fear, and it was effective, making it nearly impossible to escape.

The estate on the left had a majestic, immaculate temple, the envy of any architect. A tall steeple reached toward the heavens with a golden angel heralding a horn on the top. The grounds were immaculate, as were their members. Everyone smiled and appeared to be happy. They were really good people who did very good things. They are nice!

On the other parcel was a mighty-looking watchtower. Hundreds of old wooden circular treadmills surrounded the structures. These treadmills were invisible but tangible to those who joined the organization. On each treadmill were two members called "Publicists" walking in circles, side by side. They were working very hard to earn something, and they were relentless. Finally, orders were broadcast from the tower on schedule, and a new team marched out to begin a shift, rehearsing their drilled-in lines along the way.

Faithful told Chris that his grandmother belonged to the organization that owned the tower. She worked hard her entire life, hoping to secure a place in *paradise*. "I could tell she was always fearful, never sure Jehovah would accept her. I tried to show her this passage from The Book." **He saved us, not on the basis of deeds which we have done in righteousness, but according to His mercy."** Titus 3:5

"How did she respond?" Chris asked.

"Not well," answered *Faithful*, "She pridefully brushed me aside, saying, 'Son, you do not understand that Book.'"

Chris, now perplexed, said, "I've read where both King David

A Different Gospel

and the Apostle Paul proclaimed in The Big Book; **For ALL have sinned and fallen short of the glory of God."** "And **There is NONE righteous, not even one.** *Romans 3:23*

"So, it's clear that anyone who thinks they can obtain holiness on their own has chosen the antithesis of God's conditions for redemption. Therefore, they rejected the *Free Gift* and canceled Christ's sacrifice on the cross!"

Faithful added, "Yeah, and what about the thief on the cross next to Jesus. *The Lord* said to him. **'Truly, I say to you, today you will be with me in Paradise.'** *Luke 23:43*

Just moments before his death, this thief recognized who Jesus truly was. Then he made this request; **remember me when you come into Your Kingdom.** *Luke 23:42* He had no time to earn or be good for his salvation; but only to confess he was a sinner and believed in Christ, the Son of God.

They have twisted passages in The Big Book to convince themselves that Christ *only* made it possible to **work out your salvation with fear and trembling.** *Philippians 2:12-13*
https://www.gotquestions.org/fear-and-trembling.html

"This deception is enough to send anyone into eternity without redemption. They teach that the concept of **calling on the name of the Lord and you will be saved** *Romans 10:13* is too simplistic; this thing called *grace* is the easy way out!

"However, God does require something from us, which is difficult for many. Regardless of how good we think we've lived; we must look in the mirror and acknowledge what The Big Book says about us. **For all of us have become like one who is unclean, And all our righteousness are like filthy garments.** *Isaiah 64:6* Therefore, whoever comes to *The Lord* must swallow their pride, regardless of how good they believe they've lived, and admit to their wretched condition. Then receive Jesus into their heart as *Lord* and *Savior.* For He, and only He, is **The Lamb of God who takes away the sins of the world!"** *John 1:29*

Chris said to *Faithful,* "If it were true that humans can be reconciled to a Holy God through their efforts, then **Christ died needlessly.** *Galatians 2:21* Good works are the fruits of our salvation, and by no means, the condition."

Exhilarated with the conversation, *Faithful* knew they were

A Different Jesus, a Different Spirit

fulfilling this passage from The Big Black Book. **Always be prepared to give an answer to everyone who asks you to give the reason for the hope that you have. But do this with gentleness and respect.** *1 Peter 3:15*   And, **We are no longer to be tossed here and there by waves and carried about by every wind of doctrine, by the trickery of men, by craftiness in deceitful scheming.** *Ephesians 4:14*

"So, you see, Chris, these organizations are master manipulators; they expertly train their flock that being a subject of their organization is the *only* way. And that only they possess the truth; however, their truth is (the organization), not Jesus Christ!

"They have replaced Jesus Christ, *The Way, The Truth,* and *The Life,* with their allegiance to their organizations. Therefore, you are not saved, redeemed, or destined for the *Promised Land* or *Paradise* if you're not a member.

"This is why The Book gives us very sober warnings." *Faithful* opened The Big Book and read, **"See to it that no one takes you captive through philosophy and empty deception, according to the traditions of men, according to the elementary principles of this world, rather than according to Christ."** *Colossians 2:8*

Chris responded to Faithful. "I'm enjoying this discussion, and no doubt my sword is much sharper than before!"

Faithful was on fire and continued exposing the deceit. "You know, Chris, both organizations proclaim to be the *True Church,* preaching the *True gospel*. What's perplexing is they believe their members cannot understand The Big Book alone but only through the eyes of their prophets. They have added, changed, and taken away from The Big Book to make it conform to their man-made religion. This also happened in the early church, prompting a warning from the Apostle Paul to the church in Galatia, recorded in The Big Book."

Faithful paused for a swig of water, then continued. "Chris, listen to this! **I am amazed that you are so quickly deserting Him who called you by the grace of Christ for a different gospel. Which is really not another; only some are disturbing you and want to distort the gospel of Christ.** *Galatians 1:6* "And this! **But even though an angel from heaven or we preach a gospel contrary to what we have preached to you, let him be accursed. As we have said**

before, I say again, if any man is preaching to you a gospel contrary to what you have received, let him be accursed." *Galatians 1:8*

With a grim face, Chris responded. "*Faithful,* this is serious stuff, and the ramifications are grave and eternal! Let him be accursed! And all the while, they sincerely believe they own the truth."

Faithful had more to say. "You're right, Chris! These newly conceived religions began in the eighteen hundreds in America a short time ago. And since they claimed they are *the true church,* a conflict was created by default. What happened in the hundreds of years, from the end of the early church to the establishment of these new religions?"

"Yeah, that's right!" Exclaimed Chris. "That would mean that God went silent all those years and that no one knew *The Truth,* leaving the millions of people during that time in the darkness! It doesn't make sense!

"Jesus told His apostles to spread the *Good News* throughout the earth. Did He change His mind and turn off the light? Nonsense! I don't believe it for a second!" History records millions who loved and followed *The Savior;* many of them were put to death. All before these two man-made religions came into existence. How can their members not see this?"

Then *Faithful* shared a well-hidden fact with Chris. "The second prophet from the temple grounds made this shocking claim that attacked the very foundation of our faith. He said, *"The sacrifice made on the cross by Jesus Christ in the form of His own blood was ineffective for cleansing some sins.* This delusional false prophet, Brigham Young, continued concerning adultery; *"The blood of Christ will never wipe that out; your own blood must atone for it."* _Journal of Discourses, 3:247; 4:219-220_

Chris jumped in heatedly. "That is blatantly false! The Big Book plainly states **The blood of Jesus His Son cleanses us from All sin.** *1 John 1:7* And, **if we confess our sins, He is faithful and righteous to forgive our sins and cleanse us from ALL unrighteousness."** *1 John 1:9*

Faithful remarked, "Chris, even within our own family, I've witnessed some become enamored with polished, charismatic leaders and churches. Sadly, some of the *King's* children put these 'spiritual giants' on a pedestal."

That's true! Chris interjected. "It's regrettable; what's evident is that they have placed a church, priest, pastor, or teacher on the throne, where only Jesus should sit."

Faithful added. "It's a serious problem and a form of idolatry. Even the Apostle Paul had to correct the Corinthian church, who did the same. **Each one of you is saying, "I am of Paul," and "I of Apollos," and "I of Cephas," and I of Christ." Has Christ been divided? Paul was not crucified for you, was he? Or were you baptized in the name of Paul?** *1 Corinthians 1:12* And like the children of Israel who begged for a King, they wanted an earthy ruler between God and them. So, God gave them what they wanted, and consequently, the nation suffered."

Chris told *Faithful*, "We've learned a lot; we should move on before the sun sets."

So, they continued up the path until their silhouettes disappeared. The two monumental structures remained firmly planted on each side of *The Way.* Their members lie in wait to alter the direction of naive believers.

It's been a long day, so Chris and *Faithful* found a serene field near a lake full of crystal-clear water. Anticipating a long-awaited wash, they rushed to the edge and pulled off their boots.

"You know, *Faithful*," Chris remarked, I will remain suited up, just in case."

With a sigh of relief, *Faithful* said, "Yes, that would be wise; God forbid we both get caught without our armor!"

Chris recalled a warning from The Big Book, **Be sober in spirit, be on alert. Your adversary, the devil, prowls about like a roaring lion, seeking someone to devour.** 1 Peter 5:8

Chris sensed these parts of the woods were dangerous; *who knew what was lurking out there*? So, he sat on a boulder and kept guard while *Faithful* relaxed in the lake.

Chris's mind wandered to the many insights he'd discovered in such a short time. One passage from The Book turned his world upside down, changing his perspective on everything. **For the things seen are temporal, but the things not seen are eternal.** 2 Corinthians 4:18

Chris ruminated. *I've spent my entire life focusing on the physical world, thinking, If I can't see something, it doesn't exist. But I never understood that the invisible world has power over the physical world!* **For our struggle is not against flesh and blood, but against the rulers, against the powers, against the world forces of this darkness, against the spiritual forces of wickedness in the heavenly places.** Ephesians 6:12 **For the mind set on the flesh is death, but the mind set on the Spirit is life and peace. Set your mind on the things above, not on the things on earth.** Romans 8:6

This is a crazy new reality I've had to adapt to since I entered His kingdom. From now on, I must see everything through different eyes and a different mind, **the mind of Christ.** *1 Corinthians 2:16*

Faithful slapped Chris on the back, snapping him from his thoughts. "Your turn, buddy!"

Faithful built a campfire and prepared dinner while Chris swam in the lake. The night was peaceful; the wind slowly flowed through the trees. Chris and *Faithful* stared at the glistening stars for a while, then *Faithful* broke the silence.

"You know, Chris, King David was gifted when he expressed his thoughts; it's as if he was articulating my thoughts."

"What do you mean?" asked Chris.

"Listen to this; **When I consider Your Heavens, the works of your fingers, the moon, and the stars which you have set in place; What is man that You are mindful of him?** *Psalms 8:3* As I gaze into the heavens, these are my thoughts too!"

"You're right," replied Chris, "Mine as well, and it's also written that He loves and cares for us, even though we seem so tiny and insignificant. In moments like this, our *King's* existence becomes crystal clear. Not only did He create the Heavens and the Earth, but even now, He holds it all together by His magnificent power. Listen to this from The Big Book!" **And He *(Christ Jesus)* is the image of the invisible God, the firstborn of all creation. For *by Him*, all things were created, both in heaven and on earth, visible or invisible; <u>all things</u> <u>have been created by Him,</u> <u>and for Him.</u> And He is before all things, and <u>in Him, all things hold together.</u>** *Colossians 1:15*

Awed by this passage, *Faithful* remarked, "Let that soak into your gray matter!"

Chris replied. I must agree with King David, who said, **The fool has said in his heart, There is no God.** *Psalms 14:1*

They both agreed that *The King* is glorious, magnificent, and mighty. They praised and thanked Him, then fell asleep.

Chapter 11
Vanity Fair

They rose early and continued their journey in high spirits. *Faithful* told Christian about his years as a bricklayer. He enjoyed building churches, homes, walls, and fireplaces of brick, block, and stone. "You know, Chris, there was such a feeling of accomplishment at the end of the day, standing back and looking at my work. Then coming home tired, knowing I had provided for myself and my family. That, too, is a blessing from God!"

Chris responded, "*Faithful,* my career as a defense lawyer was much different. One day, I would come home happy, knowing that I had saved an innocent person from years of imprisonment. But, the next day, I was angry and frustrated after making up falsehoods that resulted in a guilty criminal going free and repeating his crime on another.

"Then I came across a passage in The Big Book that sent chills up and down my spine. '**Woe to you lawyers as well! For you weigh men down with burdens hard to bear, while you yourselves will not even touch the burdens with one of your fingers.** '" Luke 11:46

Faithful responded, "Yes, Chris, defending the innocent is like a calling, and the reward must be overwhelming. However, knowingly getting a lawbreaker off free places a heavy burden on the victims and their families. However, you can walk away from that burden once the verdict is declared. You must struggle with that now that you've committed to *The Holy One.*"

Chris agreed. "I do wrestle with that, and I know what The Big Book says will happen. **So, then each one shall give an account of himself to God.** Romans 14:12 I know these offenders will eventually be judged and sentenced. But still, I want no part in their wickedness any longer. Their only hope is Christ."

Suddenly, there was a change in scenery. They noticed litter along both sides of *The Way*. Nasty magazines, empty beer cans, vodka bottles, and even spots where massive amounts of food and alcohol were up-heaved. Scattered among the litter were large Black Books. *Faithful* stepped off the path and picked one up. "Chris, this is what I feared; these are our *King's Big Black Books*. This is like that field along the path *ole Worldly Wiseman* advised you to follow!"

"What do you make of it?" Chris asked.

Faithful gave his unfiltered opinion. "Many of *The Lord's* children eventually pass through the likes of *Vanity Fair*. And instead of preparing to resist temptation, they become weak, choosing fun and forbidden pleasure. So, they set aside their allegiance to our *King* and block out what they know of His commands. In truth, they toss away *His word*.

All His children have faced this struggle throughout time, that includes you and me! And when we face those occasions, we have a choice; engage in the pleasures of sin, or remain faithful to *The King*.

Moses grew up in Egypt, and when he became a man, he made a courageous decision. **Choosing rather to endure ill-treatment with the people of God, than to enjoy the passing pleasures of sin.** Hebrews 11:25 Moses acted on faith and obeyed, believing that God's reward would exceed the treasures of Egypt."

Christian asked. "How can we, *His children*, choose the momentary pleasure of sin, knowing who we are, and whom we represent?"

Faithful answered, "As you know, **the spirit is willing, but the flesh is weak.** That's why He instructs us to; **Keep watching and praying that you may not enter into temptation.** *Matthew 26:41*

"Since the fall of man, humans have devised clever arguments to justify engaging in behaviors that are off limits by our *King*. Some will twist the scriptures to convince themselves that their behavior is *no big deal,* an exception made especially for them. Regardless, the outcome is always the same, alienation from *The King*. Thus, those who have cast their Big Books have become the people spoken of in this passage; **Do you not know that friendship with the world is hostility towards God? Therefore, whoever wishes to be a friend of the world makes himself an enemy of God."** *James 4:4*

Chris mentioned to *Faithful* that he was getting a heavy feeling.

Shortly after, outrageous billboards displayed colorful, bright, sensual images that pulled the eyes from the sockets. Chris and *Faithful* were fighting to keep their minds on *The Lord*. One sign read: WELCOME TO VANITY FAIR, WHERE THERE'S NO MEASURE TO YOUR PLEASURE!

Faithful became concerned, then asked, "Do we have to walk through this sleaze?"

"I'm afraid so," replied Chris. **"We are in the world, but are not of the world,** *John 15:19* and, **we have become aliens and strangers** *1 Peter 2:10* **walking in a world that lies under the power of the evil one.** *1 John 5:19* We have no choice; we must travel through this place. However, if we follow the warnings and instructions of our *Lord*, we'll be okay!"

Chris and Faithful sat and rested under a tree. Chris read from his Big Book. "**Do not love the world, nor the things in the world; if anyone loves the world, the love of the Father is not in him. For all that is in the world, the lust of the flesh and the lust of the eyes and the boastful pride of life is not from the Father but from the world. And the world is passing away, and its lusts, but the one who does the will of God abides forever."**
1 John 2:15

Faithful made eye contact with Chris, and they both nodded in agreement with the words of truth they just heard.

After an afternoon snooze in the shade, Chris rose and jabbed *Faithful*. "You ready?" *Faithful* yawned and replied, "Yes, let's get through this!" So, the two determined soldiers set a fast pace, keeping their eyes forward.

Finally, at nightfall, they arrived in the town square; the crowd was chaotic. Everyone had become unconstrained, convinced they were liberated and having fun. Women defied modesty and flaunted their erotic behavior. Vulgarities spewed from the mouths of arrogant young men and women who believed they were cool. Parades of every kind flaunted their perversions publicly with pride. Drunks wandered the streets, boasting and fighting. Young and old addicts shoot up in the alleys. They're all here for a good time.

Like *Destruction City*, the pretense displayed in *Vanity Fair* was brazen. A never-ending herd of people, coming and going, pretending to be sophisticated and happy. Young adults come to celebrate adulthood in lewd ceremonial acts defying any boundaries of decency. Open orgies are there for anyone's entertainment, enjoying life's pleasures. Men behaved like animals, loud, crude, and boastful. They sought to exhibit worldliness, a fake manliness; however, they only proved that they were a poor excuse for a man.

Women who were lewd, loud, and lusty; endeavored to look shy. While others who are shy, naive, and innocent try to look lewd, loud, and lusty. Pimps mingled through the crowds offering incredibly young girls. Peddlers passed out pornographic advertisements offering live exhibitions of every vile sexual act that defied any description.

Under a smokescreen of enlightenment, these people considered themselves part of an advanced, tolerant new-age civilization. A progressive, liberated, and affluent society indulging in the ceremonial putrid filth *Vanity Fair* offered. However, like a chameleon they change colors when they return home, heralding deep concern for their "children's future."

Chris and *Faithful* became boxed in by those celebrating every conceivable worldly vice. The sounds of demonic spirits whooshed over their heads, whispering foul, lustful temptations.

People everywhere, attempting to be funny, said the same things; "What happens in *Vanity Fair* stays in *Vanity Fair*." But, of course, Chris and *Faithful* recognized this was a destructive lie. They knew debauchery left a lasting mark that stained the soul and haunted the conscience. They looked at each other, relaying the same thought; *this is absurd!*

Finally, Chris and *Faithful* squeezed into a casino lobby, looking for a place to sit. The lasciviousness continued as Chris and *Faithful* watched in astonishment. Inside the glistening golden buildings were lustful-looking women in bunny costumes. They weaved in and out, keeping the patrons intoxicated while they liberally fed money into the playground coffers. Old women hypnotically floated from one machine to the next, holding a yummy cocktail while a cigarette dangled loosely from their lips. All were searching for the lucky machine to make them rich, happy, and gratified; none were true.

Then, an attractive young woman staggered over and stood before Chris and *Faithful*.

"Hi, fellas, my name is *Sorrow;* you mind if I sit here?" Chris answered. "Sure, have a seat!"

Unexpectedly, *Sorrow* began sobbing. "I don't know what to do!" Chris and *Faithful* became wide-eyed and hesitant. Finally, Chris asked her, "Do you want to talk about it?"

She turned her head and answered. "Yes!"

Chris took the lead and asked, "What's troubling you?"

Sorrow gained her composure and then began. "I'm pregnant, and I don't know what to do. When I told my boyfriend, he pulled away from me and went to be with another. I thought he loved me!"

Sorrow paused to weep, then continued. "My friends tell me to get an abortion, but it makes me cringe when I think about that. They say no one has the right to tell me what to do with my body and not to worry; it's not a person, only a blob of tissue, a fetus! But I can't get it out of my head; I have a helpless innocent baby growing inside me who also has a body with a heartbeat. Who's going to defend this baby's rights?

And then, according to my so-called friends, the most

Sorrow

important thing was to make sure I proclaim my right to do with my body what I want!" There's something diabolical about their stance; it feels so wrong!"

Sorrow continued revealing her problems, then realized she was dumping her troubles on strangers. "I'm sorry, guys, I've had too much to drink."

Chris responded, "Don't worry about it."

Faithful quickly assured her that this moment was no accident. *Sorrow* tearfully declared that her life was ruined. Then, *Faithful* read from his Big Book. **God causes all things to work together for good to those who love God, to those who are called according to His purposes.** Romans 8:28

Then Christian asked *Sorrow*, "Do you love God?" She could not answer. So, Chris and *Faithful* shared their stories and how she, too, could lose her burdens and discover direction, healing, and purpose.

Faithful consoled her. *"Sorrow,* I know it's difficult to believe in something you cannot see or touch; however, that does not prove the unseen doesn't exist. **God is a spirit, and those who worship Him must worship in spirit and truth.** John 4:24

Sorrow, you are also a spirit; I'm confident you can sense His presence. Listen to this promise from our *Savior* in The Big Book. **He who believes in Me, as the scriptures said, From his innermost being shall flow rivers of living water.** John 7:38 He's alive, and this promise is for you; if you turn into the outstretched arms of *The Prince of Peace."*

Unbeknown to Chris and *Faithful* was an elite-looking older couple perched in the corner glaring at them. Their names were *Mr. & Mrs. Snoops*, and they mingled with the echelons of academia. They grew ears, yearning to hear anything that violated their reformed sensitivities.

The Snoops looked down their noses at the working class, tagging them as uneducated, simple-minded, and naive. They clung to all the "newly created" social norms that flowed down from the higher-ranking elites they idolized. Those willing to join this cult developed several characteristics: hypersensitivity, indignation, and dishonesty. They became the accusers of the unwashed.

The latest trend was learning how to be offended. It was pretty exhausting! They believed that to be considered *enlightened,* they must seek occasions to be offended by any perceived injustice, which only they defined. But, unfortunately, *the Snoops* became very good at this new behavior and were proud of their notoriety.

Now, Chris and *Faithful* offended them for publicly pushing their religion on a vulnerable young woman. Unable to control their indignation, they called the police.

The Snoops

Within minutes, two officers marched up to Chris and *Faithful,* then asked, "What do you think you're doing?"

Faithful answered. "We were talking and praying with this young woman. Have we done something wrong, officers?"

Not liking *Faithful's* tone, one officer responded, "Look here, smarty-pants. Yes, it's illegal. You can't have any religious activities in a public forum! And the owner of this establishment is offended by such behavior and forbids it!"

Chris and *Sorrow* watched as *Faithful* dug in his heels. "Officers, we have been respectful and discreet; besides, you don't seem bothered with those shouting vulgarities and behaving rudely throughout this casino!"

So, to impress his "enlightened" superiors, *Officer Bootlicker* loudly announced, "Okay, sir, stand up! I'm placing you under arrest for being a public nuisance!"

Faithful complied and allowed the officers to handcuff him; then, they marched him to the police station. The officers told Chris to attend court in the morning, where *Faithful* would appear before the *Honorable Judge Hategood.*

Chris and *Sorrow* were shaken, so they searched for a secluded place to sit and talk. Finally, out of sight of *the Snoops, Sorrow* spoke up. "I've never witnessed anything like that before, it's like good versus evil, and evil is winning!"

"Yes, *Sorrow,* it's called spiritual warfare, and it's manifested when anyone comes close to surrendering to *The Lamb of God."*

Chris encouraged *Sorrow,* "*The Savior* is knocking on the door of your heart; let Him in. If you do, you will be set free from your burden. However, you must admit that you are a sinner. If you let Him in, you will discover the peace, joy, and love you have desperately craved."

Sorrow hugged Chris; then they withdrew to their rooms.

Meanwhile, *Faithful* was locked up in a cell with druggies, drunks, prostitutes, thieves, and thugs. He was repulsed by the stench and looked for some space; however, the police continued locking up more offenders. *Lord, why is this happening to me? But,* like so many times before, several passages from The Big Book appeared in his mind. **Is it not those who are well who need a physician, but those who are sick? I have not come to call the righteous but sinners to repentance.** *Mark 2:17* **Conduct yourselves with wisdom towards outsiders, making the most of the opportunity. Let your speech always be with grace,**

seasoned, as it were, with salt, so that you may know how you should respond to each person. Colossians 4:5 *Faithful* had his answer, so he began sharing the *Good News* with anyone who would listen.

The following morning, *Faithful* waited in the courtroom for *Judge Hategood*. Chris sat anxiously in the back when the door opened, and *Sorrow* stepped in. Chris signaled to her to sit with him. While waiting for the Judge, Chris asked, "What made you come here?"

"*Faithful* wouldn't be here if it weren't for me." Replied *Sorrow*

Yes, that's true *Sorrow*; however, just know that God allowed it, so don't feel bad."

Then Chris noticed from the corner of his eye *Mr. & Mrs. Snoops* lurking in the back row glaring at them with contempt.

It was evident by the looks on their faces that they were eager for the severest sentence for *Faithful*.

Sorrow told Chris, "When I got to my room, I fell to my knees in remorse and cried out to God. It was such a strange and emotional experience. I was talking with God; my eyes were closed, and I saw myself lying at the foot of the cross. Then the blood of Jesus began to flow over me; it was warm and cleansing. Words came to me, 'Daughter, rise; your sins are forgiven.' Chris, this may sound fabricated to some, but it's true. I've never felt this much peace and joy in my entire life. It's like someone is watching over me and caring for me. I just had to come here and thank you and *Faithful* for your courage in sharing with me, *The Truth*."

Amazed, Chris answered. "You know, *Sorrow*, your story was not fabricated. The *Spirit of God* can move any way He wants, and what you've told me is precisely what *The Big Book* describes when anyone comes to Christ, and is born again. So here, listen, these are the words of Jesus."

Chris read from his *Big Book*. "**Truly, truly, I say unto you, unless one is born again, he cannot see The Kingdom of God. That which is born of the flesh is flesh, and that which is born of the spirit is spirit. Therefore, do not marvel that I said to you, you must be born again.**"
John 3: 3, 6 & 7

Sorrow could barely contain herself. "That's it, Chris, I was born again, but this time, of the spirit!"

Invigorated, Chris continued. "Yes, there's more! **For God did not send the Son into the world to judge the world, but that the world should be saved through Him.**" *John 3:17*

Suddenly, the door opened, and the bailiff announced, "All rise, the *Honorable Judge Hategood* presiding."

Faithful peeked back to locate Chris, and they exchanged looks of concern.

Bang, bang, sounded the gavel. The Judge was serious-looking, with wrinkled lines surrounding his mouth that revealed the absence of a smile. His eyes were dark and stern. The bailiff cleared his throat, then announced, "Case number 666, the people of *Vanity Fair* vs. *Faithful*. Will the defendant rise!"

Faithful stood alongside his court-appointed attorney. The man spent less than five minutes with him before the hearing, and he reeked of whiskey.

This isn't looking good, Faithful thought.

So, *Judge Hategood* began, "Mr. *Faithful*, you're charged with being a public nuisance. How do you plead?"

Judge Hategood

"Not Guilty, your honor." The Judge scoffed.

Faithful seated himself and waited for his attorney to stand up and present his defense. Silence filled the room when finally, *Mr. Whiskey* began snoring. *Faithful* rolled his eyes and raised his hand.

"Stand," demanded *Hategood*.

Faithful jumped up. "Your honor, as you see, my defender is in no condition to proceed, so I'm requesting my friend, Christian, to represent me."

Unable to deny the obvious, the judge ordered the bailiff to remove *Mr. Whiskey* from the courtroom. Chris came forward and began his defense. First, he told the Judge that the "public nuisance" charge was false. And that the only disorder, in this case, was committed by *The Snoops*, who didn't mind their own business.

From the back of the room came gasps from the offended *Snoops*. *Judge Hategood* was annoyed but allowed Chris to continue.

"Your honor, the highest law in the land, the Constitution, allows free speech, and no law states where free speech is prohibited. Furthermore, there has been precedence that our Congress opens each session with prayer, even in a government building! How much more should we citizens have the freedom to pray in public? Therefore, your honor, I move that these charges be dropped."

Chris sat down next to *Faithful* and waited for *Judge Hategood's* ruling.

Then, *Hategood* spoke. "While it is true that the charge of public nuisance is extreme, I find the inconsiderate nature of this public discourse highly insensitive. Therefore, *Faithful*, I sentence you to one month of probation. You will attend *sensitivity classes* five days per week during your probation. I hope you will reevaluate the incredible beliefs you've chosen to sell to others. And that you will refrain from that nonsense in the future!"

Chris jumped up. "Your honor, with all due respect, is your ruling based on constitutional law that protects our freedom of speech and religion? Or is it a decision based on current popular progressive vogues?"

Infuriated with Chris's boldness, *Judge Hategood* slammed the gavel down and pronounced, "Court adjourned!" Chris, *Faithful*, and *Sorrow* left the courtroom. On the way out, they spotted *The Snoops* glowing with glee.

They walked from the court building onto the walkway.

Vanity Fair had calmed down; the masses were recuperating from their activities the night before. Then, Chris finally spoke. "Wow, that was unjust and predisposed! We need to get out of here. Let's head to the edge of town; there's a church where we can get some help."

They collected their belongings and left. *The Evil Empire* faded in the distance as they approached a timeworn church nestled in the trees. The millions who suffered the likes of *Vanity Fair* often traveled to this humble dwelling. Those whose backpacks were filled with guilt, hurt, depression, rejection, and pain; came seeking *Comfort, Guidance,* and refuge. Now three more casualties have arrived. An older couple, *Comfort* and *Guidance*, sat together outside as if they were expecting them.

Chris began, "Hello, please remain seated. My name is Christian, and these are my friends, *Sorrow* and *Faithful*." But before Chris could say any more, *Comfort* rose and embraced *Sorrow*. Chris and *Faithful* went silent, astonished by *Comfort's* keen perception.

Comfort spoke, "Come, my dear, let's go inside."

Then *Guidance* stood, and with a deep voice, said, "Gentlemen, come, let's join them." They entered the church where the presence of *The Holy One* could be felt in the air, like a breeze that came and went. So, without a word spoken, the three bathed in peace. Everyone took a seat in the foyer, then *Mr. Guidance* said softly. "Praise God; what brings you to this place today?"

Faithful, Chris, and *Sorrow* told of their dreadful episodes in *Vanity Fair. Comfort* and *Guidance* were well prepared to deal with the consequences of *the land of pleasure.*

He began with *Faithful.* "*Faithful,* you can stay in the cottage

Comfort and Guidance

behind the church until your probation ends. Meanwhile, you can earn your keep by maintaining the grounds.

Now, concerning these *sensitivity classes,* the name is a ruse. The more accurate description is *re-education training;* the purpose is to control thought and speech. Behind this manipulation is a powerful group of deceitful elitists who have christened themselves as the arbitrators of social truths and norms to which we must conform. In short, they are *Thought Police;* however, their thoughts are controlled by the **god of this age.** *2 Corinthians 4:4*

Memorize the words of our *Savior* spoken to those who rejected Him. **You are of your father the devil, and you want to do the desires of your father. He was a murderer from the beginning and does not stand in the truth** because there is no truth in him. Whenever he speaks a lie, he speaks from his own nature, for he is a liar and the father of lies.** *John 8:4*

Faithful, do not listen to or believe them; they are liars like their father. All truth and social norms come from God and are written in The Big Black Book. So do not lose heart; soon, this will be behind you, and you can continue on *The Way.*"

Faithful took a deep breath and said, "Thank you!"

Guidance moved his attention to *Sorrow*. "Welcome to the family! You're a child of our *King*, young and vulnerable. The evil one will try relentlessly to throw you off the path. *Sorrow,* It's crucial you understand what has happened and how our *Heavenly Father* sees you.

Guidance opened The Big Book, then read aloud. **"But God, being rich in mercy, because of His great love with which he loved us, even when we were dead in our transgressions, made us alive together with Christ (by grace you have been saved) and raised up with Him, and seated us with him in the heavenly places, in Christ Jesus.** *Ephesians 2:4*

Sorrow, Jesus loves you and will provide, but make sure you put Him first. **Seek first His kingdom and His righteousness; and all these things shall be added to you."** *Matthew 6:33*

You now live in *His Kingdom.* Therefore, **do not be conformed to this world, but be transformed by renewing your mind, that you may prove what the will of God is, that which is good and acceptable and perfect.** *Romans 12:2* Lastly, **Rejoice always; pray without ceasing; in everything give thanks; for this is God's will for you**

in Christ Jesus." *1 Thessalonians 5:17*

Sorrow, the time has come for you to change your name. What do you think? Would *Joy* be a suitable replacement?"

With her eyebrows raised and a broad smile, *Sorrow* replied. "Yes, *Guidance*, I would like that very much. From now on, my name is *Joy!*"

She stepped forward and tearfully embraced *Guidance.* He kissed her head, as a father would his daughter, then said. "*Joy,* we have a safe house for women and mothers; you can stay here until you're ready to move on."

Joy enjoyed the sound of her new name and cried, "Thank You!"

Guidance turned to Chris. "You must continue your journey. You will be alone again but know that He is with you. You have been called and set apart to be an ambassador for *The King,* proclaiming **Jesus Christ is the world's light."** *John 8:12*

Fear swept over Christian, making him shrink back. "*Guidance,* I'm not qualified to serve *The King*. I have had so many failures in my past; even now, I'm tempted by evil. I am a weak man!"

"Calm down, Chris. Have you not read of King David? He, too, was weak. First, David committed adultery and then had Bathsheba's husband killed. After that, he attempted to cover up his transgression and live as if nothing had happened. But then, it all caught up to him. David paid a heavy price. However, he repented. Listen to this from The Big Book, **The Lord has sought out for Himself a man after His own heart.** *1 Samuel 13:14* Chris, that man was David!

Our *King* has used flawed men and women to carry out His purposes from beginning to end. Chris, you are qualified!

Meditate on this. **But God has chosen the foolish things of the world to shame the wise, and God has chosen the weak things of the world to shame the things which are strong.** *1 Corinthians 1:27* Christian, do not fear what you will say when you are representing our *King*. Instead, walk in the spirit, and rest assured that He will give you words of wisdom for every appointment that awaits you. Here's your promise from the *Lord*, recorded in The Big Book; **do not worry about how or what you are to say; for it will be given you in that hour what you are to say. For it is not you who speak, but** *the Spirit of your Father* **speaks in you.** *Matthew 10: 18-20* Christian, *The King* will use you."

Taken back, Chris took a deep breath, then exhaled, releasing his fear. Now, assured that this was *The King's* plan, he joined *Faithful* and *Joy*, who were experiencing a sense of well-being and direction.

They sat down for dinner and enjoyed each other's company, ending the day with thankfulness. At the break of day, everyone was up, ready to pray for Chris and send him on his way. There was sadness in the scene, not knowing if they would meet again.

When the hugs and well wishes ended, Chris disappeared into the trees to continue his journey.

Chapter 12
Strange Encounters

Down in the pristine valley ahead, was a man walking alone. Chris picked up the pace to catch him. "Hi there! My name is Chris, and you're walking on the same path I've chosen."

Yes, I'm *Grateful,* and you and your friends are why!

"Please explain," asked Chris.

"You see, Chris, not everyone in *Vanity Fair* participates in its renowned permissive activities. Many residents are repulsed by the reputation that has stained the land. Those who control *Vanity Fair* ensure no one succeeds in cleaning up this place. The boys with the bucks are the ones who squelch any effort. The owners of these lascivious establishments are in the driver's seat; they control this community.

Between the favors, gifts, and tax revenue they generate, it's no wonder these tycoons can manipulate the leaders of *Vanity Fair.* Beginning with *Mayor Compliant,* right through our Chief of Police, *Commissioner Wink,* and the affluent prosecuting attorneys. These shrewd attorneys make sure the powers that be, remain! They are keenly aware of who puts food on their tables and are diligent in protecting the status quo.

Like you and *Faithful,* anyone perceived as a threat is swiftly corralled and marched into *Judge Hategood's* courtroom to be corrected. Jury selection is fraudulent, featuring the same friends and family of *Vanity Fair's* power brokers. No one

Grateful

has the means or power to challenge these *Titans of Tinsel Town!*

"Wow," Chris responded. "Like an invisible darkness hovering over *Vanity Fair.* The Big Black Book describes this sad scene. **And this is the judgment, that the light has come into the world, and men loved the darkness rather than the light, for their deeds were evil. Therefore, everyone who does evil hates the light, fearing that his deeds be exposed.** *John 3:19*

"And just like *Destruction City,* the place I left to start my journey, so is *Vanity Fair,* controlled by leaders who hate *The Light.*"

Grateful told Chris that *Faithful* should consider himself fortunate, getting off so easy. He had witnessed others on the same path receive the severest sentences possible. Yet, at the same time, those who are part of the establishment get a mild reprimand.

"So, Chris, I watched you and *Faithful* the entire time; I followed you into the casino and observed how you cared for *Sorrow*. Standing off in the corner was an older couple pointing at you and whispering in each other's ears. They made a phone call, and within a minute, the police showed up. Then they handcuffed *Faithful* and took him away."

"So why were you watching us?" asked Chris.

Grateful replied. "I noticed in the street among the revelers that you and *Faithful* were anxious, not fitting into the scene. And then you weaved your way into the casino. I became curious because your behavior was impressive. Then the next day, I sat in the back of the courtroom and witnessed the self-control and dignity both of you maintained during that absurd trial!"

"No kidding," Chris replied, "we had no idea you were watching; it's good we behaved ourselves. The Big Book instructs us to, **Conduct yourselves with wisdom towards outsiders.** Colossians 4:5 You never know when you're being watched!"

Grateful opened up. "Chris, as a boy, my mother and father faithfully took the family to church. I attended Sunday school, church camps, and vacation bible school during the summer. I remember asking *The Savior* to come into my heart, and then I was baptized. My parents named me *Grateful*, hoping I would always be grateful to our *Savior*. Then in my teenage years, I rebelled and became a willing participant in the vices of *Vanity Fair*. It wasn't long before my life spun out of control, and my troubles snowballed. Unable to look at myself in the mirror, I instantly blamed others for my poor decisions. My appetite for pleasure, excitement, and vanity was a dead end, leaving me empty and lonely. Consequently, I became *Ungrateful.*

"After I watched you and *Faithful,* a silent voice spoke clearly, 'Follow Me and take the same path they have taken.' It was *The Spirit of The King* speaking to me. The same *King* I knew as a boy. Although I forgot about Him, He never forgot about me."

"So, what did you do?" asked Chris.

"I ran home and found my Big Black Book. I brushed off the dust and opened it, hoping my *Lord* would speak. Staring me in the face were the perfect passages." He recited them to Chris.

Wash me thoroughly from my iniquity, And cleanse me from my sin. Make me hear joy and gladness. Create in me a clean heart, O God, And renew a steadfast spirit within me. Do not cast me away from your presence, And do not take your Holy Spirit from me. Restore to me the joy of Your salvation, And sustain me with a willing spirit. *Psalms 51:2*

With eagerness, Chris inquired further. "Then what happened?"

Grateful drew in a breath. "I dropped to my knees and prayed out loud everything I read. Now, I'm clean, my joy has returned, and once again, I'm *Grateful.* Chris, I feel like I've been released from prison!"

Chris responded, "Yes, you're right." He opened *The Big Book* and read, **If therefore the Son shall make you free, you shall be free indeed.** *John 8:36*

Grateful confirmed, "That's it, I feel free!"

Having much to discuss, they continued along *The Way*. Chris felt himself getting over *Faithful's* absence. Now, he had a new friend and brother to accompany him on the journey.

Far from *Vanity Fair,* they entered a golf course. Coming over the hill, a golf cart sped toward them. It pulled up to a thudding halt, so close it nearly knocked Chris and *Grateful* off their feet. Crowning the front of this exquisite cart was a golden nameplate sporting the names of two flamboyant brothers: *Crafty* and *Moneylove.* As if on stage, these two gaudy looking men hopped out and walked up to Chris and *Grateful.*

Crafty sounded off first. "Young men, how the heck are you? We noticed you strolling through our golf course. Are you members of the *Charlatan Country Club?"*

"No sir," answered Chris. "We're just walking through on our way to the *Promise Land."*

"The Promise Land!" reacted *Moneylove.* Unable to control himself, he blurted a scoffing laugh and then laid into Chris. "Seriously, boy, you believe in that *pie-in-the-sky* fantasy? And do you still believe in Santa Claus and the Tooth Fairy?"

Chris followed the script with a laugh. "Good one Crafty! However, if there is life after you've *kicked the bucket,* it would be prudent to take this matter seriously, *instead* of scoffing! After all, eternity never ends!" The proud brothers let Christian's words go in one ear and out the other.

Then, *Moneylove* rolled his eyes and rattled on. "Look, son, let me give you some advice. You only go around once, so it makes no sense to deprive yourself. Instead, why not spend your time gaining wealth? Then you can have nice stuff, like me! Enjoy life, and experience all the pleasures and comforts you deserve. This grueling path you're on is a ruse and

Moneylove & Crafty

distraction from the important things in life. You are wasting time, and where is your reward?"

Chris became irritated, and then *Crafty* jumped in. "Listen up, young man" ~~~ "ENOUGH!" Chris shouted. "We have names! I'm Christian, and this is my friend *Grateful!*"

Startled and embarrassed, *Crafty* apologized, then continued his spiel. "Listen, Chris, I have the opportunity of a lifetime! A solid investment in a start-up company will pay a hundredfold; however, you must decide quickly before the beginning shares are sold out!"

Moneylove reinforced *Crafty's* performance. "Yes, Chris, I've already invested $100,000, and when this comes to fruition, millions will be added to my already handsome portfolio!"

Crafty continued. "Chris and *Grateful,* let's go to the club; drinks are on me! Then, we can discuss this extraordinary opportunity to enrich you and your family."

Chris answered firmly, "Gentlemen, we will continue along *The Way;* please consider joining us. Admittedly, we, too, desire riches. However, from The Big Book, I discovered many golden nuggets of wisdom from the most intelligent One on wealth and investments, our *Creator.* "

Now curious, *Crafty* and *Moneylove* allowed Chris to continue.

"Listen, gentlemen; this is from The Big Book! **Lay up for yourselves treasures in heaven, where neither moth nor rust destroys, and where thieves do not break in or steal; for where your treasure is, there will be your heart also.** *Matthew 6:20*

Not liking what he heard, *Moneylove* launched into Chris. "So, it's back to your imaginary world! You two religious zealots are fools, be on your *Way;* good riddance!"

Crafty and *Moneylove* slid back into their cart and returned to the clubhouse. They enjoyed happy hour while discussing their contempt for Chris and *Grateful,* with periodic episodes of boasting about their wealth.

The golf course disappeared, then *Grateful* questioned Chris. "I'm confused about this whole money thing and why so many people believe that the rich are evil and antagonistic to *The Truth."*

"Well, *Grateful,* I too have wondered, knowing that we must work to provide for ourselves and our families. However, I learned a lot from The Big Book, which enlightened me. I adjusted my beliefs about people and their money. For example, this well-known passage from The Big Book states. **The love of money is a root of all sorts of evil, and some by longing for it have wandered away from the faith.** *1Timothy 6:10* You see, it's not that money is evil or even having money; it's the LOVE of money that corrupts the heart!"

Grateful nodded. "So, it's evident that *Crafty* and *Moneylove* love money; however, that does not prove that all rich people love money."

"That's true," responded Chris. "Many people make a critical assumption: the rich are greedy and stingy, and the poor are not. That's false! Everyone is susceptible to greed, the poor just as much as the rich. The poor often criticize the wealthy because of *envy*, which is also a sin!"

"Yes, I must admit this is true." *Grateful* conceded. "I've heard this expressed many times by those who want what others have! And, unfortunately, I, too, have been envious of those who have more than me; it sneaks up on you!"

"*Grateful*, many people become wealthy by following the wisdom in The Big Book.

"What do you mean?" questioned *Grateful*.

"Godly character qualities!" Chris explained. "For example, equity, punctuality, dependability, diligence, discipline, endurance, contentment, honesty, and generosity. These are just a few character qualities for success and prosperity revealed in The Big Book. So, it should be no surprise that those who practice these godly traits would prosper."

Then *Grateful* threw Chris a *knuckleball*. "There's still one passage in The Book that bothers me; Jesus said to His disciples, **Truly I say to you, it's hard for a rich man to enter The Kingdom of heaven.** Matthew 19:23

Why is that?" Chris searched for an honest response, then said, "To put it simply, it comes down to who sits on the throne of a rich man's life. If one's wealth becomes their

God, then there's a problem! Wealth without God creates a false sense of security, making people think, 'I do not need God!' Also, wealthy people fear parting with their money if they submit their lives to *The King*. Therefore, they avoid encounters that could lead to a decision to follow *The Savior*. However, the perspective changes when a rich man surrenders to *The Savior*. He learns that charity increases wealth! It's hard to grasp because it goes against our nature and doesn't make sense! However, *Grateful*, this is what our *King* has declared and promised! **Give, and it will be given to you. A good measure, pressed down, shaken together, and running over, will be poured into your lap. For with the measure you use, it will be measured to you."** Luke 6:38

Grateful shook his head, "It's like being backed into a corner, then asked, "Do you truly believe and trust Me?"

Chris agreed, "Yes, and it's still hard for me to be generous, depriving me of the joy of giving."

Satisfied with Chris's answer, *Grateful* remarked, "It all comes down to the heart; who's on the throne? *Money* or *Jesus!*"

After walking uphill for hours, bright flowers adorning the path were noticeable. Finally, they reached a spectacular plateau. Chris and *Grateful* were surrounded by fruit trees: peaches, apples, and oranges. There were pecan trees surrounded by patches of yellow flowers and plumes of Indian grass. On the horizon were mountain peaks crowned with white. The sky behind was pale blue, transitioning to indigo blue, indicating that nighttime was coming. Chris and *Grateful* were so enamored with their surroundings that they agreed to name this location *Pleasant Valley*.

"Everything is pleasant here," *Grateful* remarked.

Then, looking ahead, Chris became fascinated. *"Grateful,* look at the stream; the fish are jumping everywhere. Let's go!"

So, they broke off branches from a fallen tree, made fishing poles, and used string and safety pins. They baited their improvised hooks with worms and sat at the water's edge. Both remained silent except for a couple of whispered prayers requesting a catch for dinner.

Finally, both lines began to jerk; they dragged their prizes onto the bank with the exhilaration of young boys. And like boys, they measured to see who caught the biggest fish. Chris cleaned the fish and began cooking them over the campfire while *Grateful* gathered fruits and cool water from the stream.

Chris announced, "Time to eat!" Both had a raging appetite, so a quick prayer of thanksgiving was spoken, then they dug in.

"My goodness, that was delicious," *Grateful* said., Both leaned back on tree trunks, snacking on pecans, each reading their Big Black Book. It didn't take long before they were each snoring away, lying next to the fire.

Chris and *Grateful* experienced pleasant dreams in *Pleasant Valley* that night.

Chapter 13
Giant Despair

A new day began. Chris and *Grateful* gobbled up some fruit and then packed more for later. Once on the path, *Grateful* commented, "Chris, this journey has many enjoyable experiences, moments of happiness, and a deep sense of well-being. It's not all hardships and gloom but many miles of absolute delight!"

"You're right," Chris answered. "Jesus spoke to His disciples; **But the Comforter, the Holy Spirit, whom the Father will send in My name, He will teach you all things, and bring to your remembrance all that I said to you. Peace I leave with you; My peace I give to you; not as the world gives."** John 14:26

"Exactly, Chris, that describes this phenomenon. I feel comforted and peaceful, different than before. This is internal, not because of some external thrill or induced excitement. What Jesus told His disciples is true; *The Holy Spirit* lives in me, giving me comfort, guidance, and conviction when I've entertained evil thoughts."

"Yes," Chris added, "and when we go astray, **He is our *Shepherd* whose rod and staff comforts me."** Psalms 23:4

Hours passed, and the beauty of *Pleasant Valley* dissipated. The terrain became repulsive and arid. The path was rocky and riddled with crevices. After becoming disheartened and fatigued, they came to a small gate; it opened onto a smooth-looking trail parallel to *The Way*. With his feet and ankles throbbing, Chris stopped and told *Grateful*, "Let's take this trail; it's much smoother." *Grateful* was younger; however, he asked Chris, Are you sure about this? The Big Book tells us there is only *One Way*."

"Yeah, I know, but it runs parallel to *The Way*, so we'll be fine," Chris assured him.

Grateful shrugged and yielded to Chris's wish. They both entered the gate and began walking the smoother detour. All was going well, so Chris boasted. "You see, *Grateful*, everything is going smoothly; I told you so!"

They walked until nightfall. They could no longer see their proximity to *The Way*. Then, Chris and *Grateful* were startled when water sloshed around their ankles and knees. It was soon up to their waist. They could no longer see or feel the path under their feet. Water continued to rise, and soon they despaired for their lives.

Embarrassed and ashamed, Chris told *Grateful*, "Brother, this is all my fault! We should have remained on the original path. Please forgive me."

"It's okay, Chris; I forgive you. You've been on *The Way* longer than me, so I followed you. But don't be discouraged; our unseen guide will get us back on the path."

Grateful added, "I must always guard myself against judgment toward others! The Apostle Paul instructed us to **Be kind to one another, tenderhearted, forgiving each other, just as God in Christ also has forgiven you.** Ephesians 4:32 No doubt, the day is coming when I will ask you for forgiveness for some future foolish decision."

Chris felt better with that burden off his chest. They paused to implore the *Lord* for help, and the water quickly receded! They started walking again and finally found themselves at the little wooden gate. Weary, they made their way to higher ground, off the path. There they fell down, dog-tired, and went to sleep. As daybreak began, they were both in a deep sleep. The weather took a bad turn. Dark, ominous clouds floated through the sky, and piercing cold air settled over the countryside.

Then, abruptly, Chris and *Grateful* awakened, screaming in excruciating pain. Completely disoriented, both tried to figure out what was happening. Then a loud, gruff voice growled, and a monster of a man stood over them, kicking each of them in the stomach, back, and ribs.

"Get up!" he hissed. "Get to the castle ahead!" The fellow was so huge that his enormous, iron-like arms dealt the heaviest of blows. Severe kicks from his hobnail boots drove them forward, stumbling and falling until they rolled into a dismal *Doubting Castle*.

Inside this dark castle appeared the giant's wife, a ghastly-looking creature who shoved Chris and *Grateful* into a room, then kicked them down a flight of stone steps into a cold, damp room. The door closed with a final dreadful slam.

Sore and wounded, no words were spoken. They were overwhelmed with absolute despair and gloom, void of strength; finally, they fell asleep. They woke up continually, attempting to become comfortable, but there was a sense of helplessness. Indeed, all hope was gone!

The only break in their misery was when the door opened above, and hateful scowling faces looked down on them. These hideous monsters cackled villainous laughs that echoed down the stairwell. They snarled snide demeaning insults mixed with bombardments of accusations. Then, they injected vivid thoughts of past tragedies and failures into the minds of Chris and *Grateful*, paralyzing them in a *Cage of Despondency*.

Giant Despair & The Doubting Castle

From the beginning, this castle has been *The Victims Prison.* Built by the debauchery, depravity, and perversion of sinful men's blackened souls, untold millions have anguished within. Among the *victims* are children who fell prey to the putrid lusts of demented pedophiles. Their cries have penetrated the stone walls; they echo through the corridors pleading to be rescued. Men and women who have been betrayed by their spouses; their pain has flourished throughout the dark corridors. Here, mothers and fathers anguish, imagining their children are hopelessly lost.

Hearing the cries tormented Chris and *Grateful;* they wept in agony. And now, they question the very existence of their *King.* Lucifer's demons vomit waves of glee as they watch their victims curled up on the floor in shame, pain, confusion, and, most of all, DOUBT.

The days dragged by, alone in their *Depression.* Excluded from sunlight, Chris and *Grateful* could not measure time. They began entertaining thoughts of taking their own lives. It shook him to the core when Chris realized he wanted to end it all. Then, out of desperation, he recited from The Big Book.

"The Lord lives, and blessed be my rock; And exalted be the God of my salvation, The God who executes vengeance for me, And subdues peoples under me. He delivers me from my enemies; Surely You lift me above those who rise up against me; You rescue me from the violent man. Therefore, I will give thanks to you among the nations, O Lord, And I will sing praises to Your name. *Psalms 18: 46-49*

He slapped his forehead, then shouted, "What a fool I am!" I found this old key in my *Big Book* a while back. I've kept it in my pocket and jangled it around when I became anxious; I call it my *Promise Key.* I knew one day I would need it to open something.

Grateful replied. "What are we waiting for? Let's try it now!"

Chris and *Grateful* blindly stumbled up the steps. Then, at last, they reached the door, felt for the keyhole, and inserted it. With a turn, the lock clicked, and the door swung open. The light caused them to look away until their eyes adjusted.

Grateful stuck his head out slowly to see if anyone was guarding the corridor. "It's clear; let's go," he whispered.

They hurried from the *Doubting Castle,* running for their lives, and soon heard a commotion behind them. No doubt it was the *Big One* pursuing them.

Chris and *Grateful* returned to the path gasping for air. Bewildered from their experiences over the last week, they were now vigilant to remain on *The Way*. There was only one thing they wanted to do, recuperate.

So, they continued for a couple more hours, then discovered a safe location to spend the night. Like before, they found all the fresh water and food they needed surrounding them. Once nourished and revived, Chris and *Grateful* were eager for a discussion.

Grateful asked, "Tell me more about this *Promise Key*."

"Sure," answered Chris. "The Big Book has thousands of promises our *Almighty King* has given to His children, howbeit some, not all, are conditional based on our choices."

"Give me some examples," asked *Grateful*.

"Okay, here's one. *God is always with me.* **Have I not commanded you? Be strong and courageous! Do not tremble or be dismayed, for the Lord your God is with you wherever you go.** *Joshua 1:9*

And this one. *God will give me wisdom.* **If any of you lack wisdom, let him ask of God, who gives to all men generously and without reproach, and it will be given to him.** *James 1:5*

Here's another, *God promises us an abundant life.* **The thief comes to steal, kill, and destroy; I came that they might have life, and might have it abundantly.** *John 10:10*

The last one, *God has a plan for us.* **For I know the plans that I have for you, declares the Lord, plans for your welfare and not for calamity to give you a future and a hope."** *Jeremiah 29:11* *Grateful* could barely contain himself. "That's overwhelming! I've never seen *The Book* in this way;

these promises are mine! I'm digging in to find more of these golden nuggets."

Chris, also enthused, asserted, "You know, *Grateful*, the promises in The Big Book are inspired by God; a treasure to be discovered. Listen to this! **My son, if you receive my sayings, And treasure My commandments within you, Make your ear attentive to wisdom, incline your ear to understanding; For if you cry for discernment, Lift your voice for understanding; if you seek her as silver, And search for her as for hidden treasure; Then you will discern the fear of the Lord, And discover the knowledge of God."** *Proverbs 2:1*

The traumatic event in *The Doubting Castle* disconcerted *Grateful*. So, he changed the subject to questions he needed answered. "Chris, I believe that our *Creator* loves us, and He proved that on the cross, but there are things that bother me."

Chris handed *Grateful* some food, then leaned back on a tree. "So, what's bugging you?"

Grateful cautiously presented his questions, not wanting to appear doubtful of *The King's* love or even His existence. "How is it that a predator can strip away the innocence of a child? Why doesn't *The Almighty* prevent this? He could strike them down in a heartbeat! And why does He allow poverty, disease, starvation, and torture? Whether it's a parent losing a child, or the murder of an innocent person, people blame our *King* for these tragedies. They weep at night, crying out, why, why!" But they get no answers; I don't understand!"

Chris stopped eating and took a deep breath. "Wow, those are some heavy questions!" *Grateful* remained silent and waited for his friend to answer. Chris thought: *it will be a long night attempting to put those questions to bed.*

"First off, *Grateful*. I won't make excuses for *God Almighty*, and here's why. **But who are you, a human being, to talk back to God? "Shall what is formed say to the one who formed it, 'Why did you make me like this?** Romans 9:20

We will not understand many things until we are in His presence. **For now, we see only a reflection as in a mirror; then we shall see face to face. Now I know in part; then I shall know fully, even as I am fully known.** 1 Corinthians 13:12

However, *Grateful*, I will share what I know." Chris opened his Big Book and began. "*Grateful*, all the wickedness, corruption, fear, sickness, and death are the result of original sin, the disobedience, and rebellion of mankind against our *Maker*.

Grateful interrupted, "But what about newborns? They're innocent at birth!"

Chris quickly answered, "True; however, the entire human race is born into sin, and it takes very little time to manifest in a baby. **Surely I was sinful at birth, sinful from the time my mother conceived me.** Psalms 51:5 Sin touches our lives directly and indirectly, like cancer, it spreads, and is passed down from one generation to the next."

Grateful prodded further, "But that doesn't answer the question about protecting innocent children!"

Christian paused as he struggled to address this dark, wicked reality. "*Grateful*, there is no doubt certain sins stir up our anger more than others, this is undeniable. But when an adult sexually violates a child, that creates a fierce hatred that has no measure. And have no doubt, it stirs *The King's* wrath more! Listen to this stern warning spoken by our

Redeemer, **but whoever causes one of these little ones who believe in Me to stumble, it would be better for him to have a heavy millstone hung around his neck, and to be drowned in the depth of the sea.** Matthew 18:6

Grateful, although all sin leads to death. Christ singled out the sin of harming a child. Pedophiles *will be* judged Pedophiles *will be* punished!

Then Christian changed direction, and asked *Grateful.* "Why do you think He created us?"

Grateful answered, "I suppose since He made us in His image, it's because He wanted a relationship."

Chris stirred the campfire, then responded, "That's right, a love relationship. And that can only happen if we have free will! However, free will allows us to disobey, rebel, hate; or to love people and God. That's why He gave us His commandments, boundaries to keep us safe, and to live in peace. The only way our *Maker* could have prevented the ravages of man's rebellion would have been to create us without the freedom to choose."

Grateful remarked. "So, according to The Big Book, all the chaos surrounding us resulted from mankind's rebellion against *The King* and *His* decrees. And now we live in a corrupt world suffering the consequences of sin!"

Not just us *Grateful,* but the entire earth agonizes due to sin. This passage makes it clear. **Creation itself also will be set free from its slavery to corruption ~ for we know that the whole creation groans and suffers the pain of childbirth together until now.** Romans 8:21-22

Grateful's countenance changed. "I'm beginning to understand. If we were created without free will, we wouldn't have been made in His likeness, nor would we have had the freedom to choose good or evil. We could not have loved or hated. We would have been mindless robots."

Chris nodded his head yes, then made one final point. "I know it's hard to get our heads around this, but, *life is a gift, every day is a gift, and every breath is a gift,* and the *gift giver* is our *Heavenly Father.* However, suppose we believe that our time on earth is owed. In that case, that changes everything, especially how we respond to tragedies and death."

Grateful asked, "What do you mean?"

Chris explained, "When a person doesn't view our time on earth as *a gift,* most likely, in addition to mourning, they become angry and blame *The King* for their loss. However, if that same person acknowledges life as *a gift,* then mourning is often mixed with acceptance and gratefulness."

"I see the difference now, *Grateful* replied, "But it's still a difficult tunnel to walk through."

Chris added, "Yes, it is, and on occasions, even *The King's* children feel abandoned by Him and become angry; however, most come around, returning their trust in *The King.*"

Chris opened his Big Black Book and read. **See what great love the Father has lavished on us, that we should be called children of God! And that is what we are! The reason the world does not know us is that it did not know him.** *1 John 3:1*

Grateful, that's all I got, but rest assured that the innocent victims whose lives have ended are in a better place than us. This is what the Apostle Paul said concerning this subject. **I say and would prefer to be away from the body and at home with the Lord."** *2 Corinthians 5:8*

Still troubled over the unjust suffering of the innocent, *Grateful* understands where the blame belongs.

He takes comfort knowing that ultimately, **it is appointed for men to die once and after this comes judgment** *Hebrews 9:27* And, **Blessed *are* you who hunger now, for you shall be satisfied. Blessed *are* you who weep now, for you shall laugh.** *Luke 6:21*

Completely spent in mind, body, and spirit; they fell asleep.

Chapter 14
Just Delectable

For several days, the terrain became increasingly vivid and colorful. Delectable was the word that best defined the captivating scenery. An abundance of gardens, orchards, and vineyards surrounded Chris and *Grateful*. Countless fountains and streams waited for travelers to refresh themselves. There was a bounty of every fruit imaginable; free and delicious. Flocks of sheep grazed in pristine grass fields, watched by compassionate *Shepherds*.

Then, finally, one *Shepherd* noticed Chris and *Grateful* and began walking their way. He was an older, gentle-looking man, rugged and hefty. He reached the top of the knoll carrying a sheep over his shoulders. Then, with a smile, he said, "Good morning, young men; what brings you here?"

Chris answered. "Is this the way to *The Celestial City? The Promised Land?*"

"Yes, indeed." *The Shepherd* nodded. "You're on the right path."

"Well, how far?" asked Chris.

The gentle *Shepherd* replied, "You still have a ways to go." Then he gently lowered the sheep to the ground and said, "This fella strayed and became lost; it happens now and then, when they lose sight of *The Shepherd*."

Chris and *Grateful* looked at each other, understanding the deeper meaning of his words. Then *Grateful* asked. "Is it safe

The Good Shepherd

ahead, or are there still dangers?"

"Oh yes, it's safe if you are genuine," answered *The Shepherd*. "*Impostors* and *Pretenders* find it rough and never make it."

The Shepherd took a liking to Chris and *Grateful;* he discerned they were authentic, so he invited them to his cottage and introduced them to his three *Shepherd* brothers.

"Gentlemen, these are my brothers; *Wisdom, Instruction, Understanding,* and my name is *Knowledge*. We are responsible for the sheep who roam in the *Land of Proverbs*.

This pasture was created by *The Great Shepherd* for His sheep who travel *The Way*.

Grateful, always curious asked. "Why does this place exist"?

Knowledge The Senior Shepherd answered. "Brothers, these sheep, before entering this *Proverbial Pasture*, lived, and fed in another world their entire lives. Now they belong to *The King;* however, much of the world's philosophy and morals remained, creating conflict in their lives. And as a result, they bear no fruit. Listen to The Big Book. **For the wisdom of this world is foolishness in God's sight.** *1 Corinthians 3:19*

So, you see, a new way of living is imperative, and here's why. **Do not conform to the pattern of this world, but be transformed by the renewing of your mind. Then you will be able to test and approve what God's will is—his good, pleasing, and perfect will.** *Romans 12:2*

Grateful responded, "That makes perfect sense; If we expect to know what His will is, then we must have **the mind of Christ.** *1 Corinthians 2:16*

Shepherd Wisdom remarked. "Grateful, I discern you've been grazing in The Big Black Book!" *Grateful* received his compliment and replied, "Yes, and it's beginning to stick."

With the day ending, the brothers asked Chris and *Grateful* to stay the night; they accepted. So, After a satisfying dinner, they retired to the front porch. The sun was about to disappear behind the rolling hills blanketed with vineyards. The clouds were lined with brilliant orange, surrounded by various shades of gray.

Grateful spoke up. "Hey, everyone, let's walk over to the top of the knoll."

The Shepherds agreed. "Yes, let's watch the sunset, the end of another day."

Once on the crest of the hill, they all stood in silence, awed by the splendor that encircled them. Silhouettes of geese flew through the clear air as the sun disappeared.

Then *Shepherd Wisdom* pointed. "Look!" They caught a glimpse of something very bright, far in the distance. Scintillations of light flashed sporadically, lighting up the expanse. Not much could be said about this breathtaking moment. Instead, *The Senior Shepherd* opened his Big Book and read. "**Great is the Lord, and highly to be praised; His greatness is unsearchable. One generation shall praise Your works to another and declare Your mighty acts. On the glorious splendor of Your majesty, and on Your wonderful works, I will meditate."** *Psalms 145:3*

Shepherd Knowledge closed The Book, and they returned to the cottage to retire for the night. Christian bedded down on the front porch, then gazed into the heavens. Waiting to fall asleep, he focused on the cool night air, the sounds of the sheep and crickets. Then, finally, he fell asleep.

Chris and *Grateful* awakened to the sounds of sheep echoing from below. The three *Shepherd* brothers were in the valley tending to the flock while *Shepherd Knowledge* prepared breakfast. After breakfast, the *Shepherds* escorted Chris and *Grateful* through the vineyards, returning them to *The Way*. *Grateful* snacked on delicious juicy grapes while the *Shepherds* and Chris spoke.

While they walked together, *The Shepherds* pointed out showing side roads others had taken that led to dismal places with bleak endings. Then, finally, they arrived at the top of a hill, where they stopped and rested. *The Shepherds* pointed to the glow on the horizon.

"There it is," said Chris. This brightened everyone's mood.

Then *Shepherd Understanding* uttered. "There is *The Gate* of your destination." A wave of anticipation flowed over Christian and *Grateful* as they gazed at the bright spot beyond.

"It won't be long now," said Chris.

Grateful added, "Come on, let's get going!"

Final instructions were given. *The Senior Shepherd* said. "In the Big Black Book are *The Proverbs;* study them often and teach them to your family. These are the sayings of *The King*, **for gaining wisdom and instruction; for understanding words of insight; for receiving instruction in prudent behavior, doing what is right and just and fair; for giving prudence to those who are simple, knowledge and discretion to the young. Let the wise listen and add to their learning, and let the discerning get guidance.** Proverbs 1: 1-5

Now, one more thing. A valley between here and your destination is called *The Valley of Enchantment.* However, it should be named, *The Sea of Sorcery* because its victims drown in its spells. In that valley, the grassy fields are infested with various kinds of *Venomous Vipers.* If you are not alert, you may get bitten!"

Frightened, *Grateful* asked, "What will happen if we are bitten?"

The *Shepherd* answered, "Let's sit and talk. First, the snakes cannot slither onto *The Way*. So, do not step into the grass to keep from being bitten. However, if you wander off the trail and are bitten, it depends on which snake bites you. These venoms are different; some cause hallucinations, and some make you feel invincible. Others cause euphoria, making you feel peaceful and happy. However, they all have this in common; they are fake, temporary, and make you want to return for more. The root source comes from none other than, *The King Snake* himself, *Lucifer.* Of course, all these poisons are a substitute for what *The King of Kings* has provided through *The Holy Spirit.*

Chris questioned the *Shepherd.* "Are you telling us that *The King's* children wander off into these fields?"

"Yes, Chris, that's exactly what I'm saying. It's called temptation, a lust for fleshly pleasure, and sadly, many of His children crave these venoms. Some have become so dependent on them that they fabricate clever arguments using passages from The Big Book to justify their addictions."

Chris and *Grateful* admitted walking into these snake pits back home in *Destruction City* and *Vanity Fair.*

The *Shepherd* opened his Big Book and read. **"For the grace of God has appeared, bringing salvation to all men, instructing us to deny ungodliness and worldly desires *and to live soberly,* righteously, and godly in the present age.** Titus 2:11 & 12

Brothers, you get the point, don't get bit!"

Then, *Grateful,* always curious, asked, "Why the word *sorcery* to describe the land?"

That's an excellent question *Grateful;* it reveals that you have a *Gift* given to you from *The Great Shepherd.*"

"What *Gift* is that?" asked Grateful.

The Shepherd answered. *"Knowledge.* I believe you will soon be a teacher of The Big Black Book you carry."

Grateful was dumbfounded, having never considered that before.

The Shepherd continued with his answer. "In The Big Book, the word *sorcery* appears often. *Sorcery* is divination, spells, and communication with spirits. It's condemned and labeled a sin by our *King*. *Sorcery* is defined as evil and deceptive behavior. Now, here's the kicker! The word *sorcery* in the Big Book is the Greek word *Pharmakeia*; however, in English, it's translated, *Pharmacy*.

Chris quickly asked, "Are you making a connection between the use of drugs and *sorcery?*"

The Shepherd responded, "No, not me, but the Apostle Paul did. You see, back in his day, *sorcery* meant 'dealing in poison', or 'drug use' and pertained to casting spells. Those who practiced *sorcery* used drugs to induce *enchantments* and *curses*. Near the end of the Big Black Book is this sobering passage; **Outside are the dogs and *sorcerers* and the sexually immoral and murderers and idolaters, and everyone who loves and practices falsehood.** Revelations 22:15

Grateful, wholly enthralled, asked, "Outside of what?"

The Shepherd answered. "Outside *The Gate* of *The Celestial City."*

Chris and *Grateful* wagged their heads; they now understood the gravity of *practicing sorcery.* They stood, then Chris and Grateful expressed their gratitude and said farewell. They turned around and walked into the horizon. *The Shepherds* returned to the pasture where their sheep awaited. Now, feeling accomplished, they were ready to care for the next group of travelers.

The day was still young, Chris and *Grateful* had plenty of energy to burn, so they traveled many miles before the evening. They found a safe location and set up camp for the night. *The Shepherds* supplied them with fresh bread, grapes, and vegetables. So, with the fish they caught in a nearby pond, they enjoyed a satisfying dinner.

Afterward, they sat and talked about their recent encounters. *Grateful* said to Chris, "Our arrival into *The Celestial City* is like this double-edged sword."

"How's that?" asked Chris.

Grateful explained. "On the one hand, nothing could be better than what we will experience for eternity. But it saddens me to know that one day I will have a family of my own, and when death arrives, we will be separated. Just thinking about it grieves me."

"I understand," Chris replied, "I have those same feelings. However, I have come to terms with things I don't understand, the 'whys' of life. As it is written, **For My thoughts are not your thoughts, Neither are your ways My ways," declares the Lord. For as the heavens are higher than the earth, so are my ways higher than your ways, and My thoughts than your thoughts.** *Isaiah 55:8*

"So, you see, *Grateful*, we cannot comprehend the thoughts and ways of an infinite, all-powerful God in our present earthly form. However, we can rest assured that it will be good, an existence living in the presence of Jesus for eternity, a life without tears, pain, and evil. Here's another promise from the Big Book. **He will swallow up death for all time, And the Lord God will wipe tears away from all faces, And He will remove the reproach of His people from all the earth; For the Lord has spoken. And it will be said in**

that day, Behold, this is our God for whom we have waited; Let us rejoice and be glad in His salvation. *Isaiah 25: 8-9*

Chris assured *Grateful* that the time would come when all things would be revealed, and they would understand what they could not comprehend in the present.

"We have an awesome promise, *Grateful,* concerning our departure from this world."

"What promise?" asked *Grateful.*

Chris opened his Big Black Book and read aloud. **In My Father's house, there are many dwelling places; if it were not so, I would have told you; for I go to prepare a place for you, And if I go and prepare a place for you, I will come again, and receive you to Myself; that where I am, there you may be also.** *John 14:3*

Chris gave *Grateful* the assurance he needed. "The time will arrive when we gather together for eternity. First, with those who have crossed the *River of Death* before us, and then, those after us."

Chris and *Grateful* ended another eventful day.

Chapter 15
Family Reunion

They exited a massive gorge and stopped at the edge of the *Valley of Enchantment*. Looking down, they watched as *wayfarers* wandered aimlessly in the fields. Intoxicated with their preferred venoms, it was apparent that their journeys had come to a screeching halt.

Chris and *Grateful* looked at each other, then sat to rest before they attempted to enter the valley.

Grateful asked, "What do you think?"

First, Chris scanned the valley below and responded, "I think we need to hightail it through this valley until we get to the other side!" So, they stood up and sprinted into the valley, keeping their eyes forward. Finally, they exited, unharmed and sober.

Chris and *Grateful* congratulated each other with a handshake, then stopped for lunch and conversation, then continued on.

Up ahead, leaning against a tree, was a stern-looking man with his arms firmly crossed. His name was *Mr. Ignorant*, and he was from a small village called *Conceit*, far from *The Way*. He saw Chris and *Grateful* coming over the hilltop from the corner of his eye. When they reached *Mr. Ignorant*, they stopped and introduced themselves.

Mr. Ignorant told Chris and *Grateful* that he, too, was on *The Way* to the *Promised Land*.

Mr. Ignorant

Grateful asked, "How did you enter *The Way?*"

Ignorant responded quickly, "From a trail, I made a short way back; it connects this path to the *Village of Conceit.*"

"You mean you never entered *The Gate?*" Chris asked.

Ignorant responded with a tinge of arrogance. "Why would I take that long rough path? Plus, it's too far away!"

Grateful frowned with disappointment. "*Mr. Ignorant,* I would be concerned if I were you. The Book clarifies **Not everyone who says to Me, Lord, Lord, will enter The Kingdom of heaven; but he who does the will of My Father who is in heaven.**" Matthew 7:21

Grateful continued, "It's sad but true, many will arrive at *The Gate* of *The Promised Land,* and whether from stubbornness, conceit, or believing they make the rules; they will be turned away. If I were in your shoes, I would consider the instructions in The Big Book."

Now angry and offended, *Ignorant* cut loose. "Enough with you and that Book you hold in such high esteem! That Big Book you refer to so much is open to anyone's interpretation. So, you believe there's only *One Way* to *The Promised Land?*"

Both Chris and *Grateful* answered in harmony, "YES! Jesus proclaimed; **I AM the way, the truth, and the life; no one comes to the Father but through Me."** *John 14:6*

"Hogwash!" snapped *Ignorant*. "That's closed-minded, you fools. There are many ways to the *Promised Land.* I've got my religion, and you've got yours. You keep yours, and I'll keep mine. I'm satisfied that I'm right, and I don't need to be told I'm not following the instructions of that mildewed Book you keep referring to. Now, take that Book and be gone!"

Chris, not ready to end the exchange, spoke. *"Mr. Ignorant, The King* clearly warned us from that Book you disregard, **There is a way *which seems* right to a man, But its end is the way of death.** *Proverbs 14:12* So, please, reconsider!"

Grateful told *Mr. Ignorant* he would pray for him. *Ignorant* scoffed and brushed them away. Chris and *Grateful* continued, leaving *Ignorant* to travel his path alone.

Finally, Chris broke the silence. "You know, *Grateful,* The Big Book addresses every condition of the heart. Sadly, this passage applies to everyone who agrees with *Ignorant*. **Do you think lightly of the riches of His kindness, forbearance, and patience, not knowing that the kindness of God leads you to repentance? But because of your stubbornness and unrepentant heart, you are**

storing up wrath for yourself in the day of wrath and revelation of the righteous judgment of God. *Romans 2:4-5* *Mr. Ignorant* is in store for the shock of his *eternal life* when he shows up at *The Gate* of the *Celestial City*.

Perhaps we'll bump into him later, and he will be open."

Grateful nodded in agreement, then said a prayer for *Ignorant.*

They walked over the next hill, then stopped to refresh themselves. While sitting on the grass eating grapes, Chris looked to the other side of the path into a beautiful park that looked exactly like the one across from his home. A woman sat at the picnic table, watching her children play. Puzzled, Chris questioned himself. *Where am I? Is that my family?* He rose and walked towards them.

Grateful, unsure of what was happening, followed behind. At last, Chris recognized his wife and children. He sprinted to them, and they all embraced in a tearful reunion.

Chris introduced Angela. "*Grateful*, this is my wife, Angela."

Grateful responded, "It's a pleasure to meet you! It feels like I know you, your husband has fondly shared many stories about you.

Then, Chris continued, "I met *Grateful* along *The Way* after we exited *Vanity Fair*. We've become good friends." Angela returned the greeting, then they all sat at a picnic table.

Chris asked Angela to share how and why she began her journey. Angela reached out and held Christian's hand, then explained. "When I realized your sincerity in finding *The Way*, I regretted how I treated you and for not joining you in pursuing *The Truth*. I became ashamed, realizing I was more worried about what our family and friends would think. This made me feel weak and disloyal!

"The evening of the day you departed, I was sitting alone in the dark in my rocking chair and began reflecting on your *frustrations*. I had to admit to myself, there's indeed something wrong with the heart of humans, me included. Then I recalled my grandfather often recited this passage from The Big Book; **Men loved darkness rather than light, for their deeds were evil.** *John 3:19*

"So, I questioned myself, had my conscience been seared? Had I lost my sensitivity to evil? Then it became clear that I had become calloused to the wickedness surrounding me. Afterward, a presence covered me, conviction, and comfort all at the same time! I realized then that I, too, had a heavy burden on my back.

"The next day, I bumped into Pastor Jimmy at our town's Autumn festival; he was easy to recognize. I told him you were my husband. He remembered you and was thrilled to learn you began your journey. Then Pastor Jimmy ushered me to a private place to talk. There, I shared my experience from the night before.

"He said *The Holy Spirit* was convicting me. Then he read a passage from The Big Book. **For all of us have become like one who is unclean, and all our righteous deeds are like a filthy garment. For all have sinned and fallen short of the glory of God.** *Romans 3:23* But then Pastor Jimmy told me that **God is not willing that any perish but for all to come to repentance.** *2 Peter 3:9* And, **That God being rich in mercy, because of His great love with which He loved us, even when we were dead in our transgressions, made us alive together with Christ.** *Ephesians 2:4*

"It was at that moment my resistance collapsed, and I

surrendered. Pastor Jimmy asked if he could pray with me; I said yes. So much happened in such a short moment. First, I found myself at the foot of *The Cross,* asking *The Savior* to cleanse me of that dirty feeling. Then I witnessed a burden roll off my back into an empty grave; it was wonderful, like coming up for air! When Pastor Jimmy said, 'Amen,' all I wanted to do was give thanks and praise my new *King!*"

Astonished, Chris and *Grateful* remained silent, soaking it all in. Then, finally, they praised God. Elated that they were destined for *The Promised Land,* Christian and Angela embraced.

Several days passed, then it was time for *Grateful* to move on. Chris, however, remained with his family. A new dimension in their marriage opened up when they read The Big Book together, as they discovered golden nuggets of wisdom and truth.

Now, concerned for her children in a new way, Angela began looking for instructions from The Big Book. She discovered several verses, such as, **Train up a child in the way he should go, Even when he is old, he will not depart from it.** *Proverbs 22:6*

Eager to find more, she flipped through the pages and found another. **Let the word of Christ richly dwell within you, with all wisdom teaching and admonishing one another with psalms and hymns and spiritual songs, singing with thankfulness in your hearts to God.** *Colossians 3:16*

Chris and Angela changed their habits, family activities, and education to benefit their children. Chris spent more time playing with his children and began showing more affection and courtesy to Angela. Aware that her husband was attentive to her needs, Angela was thrilled and became more willing to care for her husband.

Although still physically joined and on the same path, Chris and Angela had their individual walks with the Lord. Now bonded together with God's favor, a new future awaited them.

The following day, Chris continued on his *Way.* Now, experiencing a surge of zeal, he anticipated a closer relationship with *The King*. To reinforce this, he repeated to himself the same passage given to him by the two ministering spirits at the cross. **"He must increase but I must decrease"** John 3:30

On *The Way* again, the sky became gray and started drizzling. Chris put on his poncho and carried on. He noticed a pitiful man ahead sitting on the path's edge, nearly in tears. The man was lamenting his tragedies and past life. *Guilt* was wrapped around this poor man so tight he could barely breathe.

Chris startled *Mr. Guilt* as he approached. "I'm sorry, sir, but I couldn't help seeing you in anguish. My name is Christian; what's your name?"

"*Guilt, Mr. Guilt*, and yes, I am in anguish. I can't go on. I'm not worthy of *The Way*. I've hurt many people, the people I love and who have helped me. I've used and deceived them because of my selfishness. I'm a disgusting example of a man!"

Chris recognized he was wallowing in remorse and self-pity, unable to forgive himself for his past. "Listen here, *Mr. Guilt*, you need to knock this off. Stand up, for crying out loud! You are letting *Guilt* rob you of your *Courage*, planting seeds of *Mistrust* in your heart. As a result, your *Faith* has become pitifully weak to the point that you won't be able to continue, making you ineffective in serving our *King*."

Chris persisted, earnestly exhorting *Mr. Guilt*.

"Look there, you've got your passport and papers in order. Get up! Shake it off! Be grateful you have those papers! Those are your legal documents pardoning you from your past and granting you passage into *The Promised Land*. *Mr. Guilt,* you must throw off who you were, where you're from, and what you have done. Isn't it true that you've been at the foot of *The Cross?*"

Guilt replied, "Yes."

"Isn't it true that you acknowledged you're a sinner, needing His forgiveness?"

Mr. Guilt nodded, "Yes."

"Then you must reject the lies you speak to yourself and start speaking the words of our *King!*" While *Mr. Guilt's* sniveling lingered, Chris opened *The Big Book* and read. **Therefore, if any man is in Christ, he is a *new creature;* the old things passed away; behold, new things have come. Do not lie to one another, since you laid aside the *old self* with its evil practices and put on the *new self* who is being renewed to a true knowledge according to the image of the One who created him.** *2 Corinthians 5:17*

"Listen to me, *Mr. Guilt!* Those papers you have are an entrance into the city, not a document to keep you out. Look here in your papers: **He has now reconciled you in His fleshly body through death, in order to present you before Him holy and blameless and beyond reproach.** Colossians1:21-22 The despairing man ignored Chris and continued lamenting and grieving with groans and tears.

Chris shook his head and continued down the path. Now traveling alone, Chris had plenty of time to think. He reflected on *Mr. Guilt* and the many others he'd encountered along the *Way*. Those who had strayed, been deceived or were vulnerable because they did not prepare for attacks from the *Father of Lies*.

This awareness caused Chris to remain humble and not think too highly of himself. He pondered. *If I'm not attentive, the same fate could befall me. I cannot become lazy, gullible, or spiritually arrogant. And any accomplishments must always be credited to God for His glory, not self-adulation.*

Chris recalled several polished ministers who became celebrities. With their perfectly fitted expensive suits and captivating smile, they performed on stage with perfect choreography, mesmerizing thousands into allegiance. These followers idolized the very ground these ministers walked on. They spoke more of their remarkable leader than of their *Savior!*

Then, when their true motives were exposed, Chris remembered how they descended into depths of *shame, embarrassment,* and *remorse. Money* and *fame* became their god. Some engaged in illicit *sex* in the darkness, testing the *Lord's* patience. Then, when the light of day revealed their nakedness, they went down in flames, leaving behind million-dollar homes, bank accounts, and church buildings. But the saddest of all was the broken lives of those who believed in and elevated these ministers. They were left disillusioned and weak.

Christian pondered. *It's astounding how so many began their journey following their unseen Guide, then decided they knew The Way better. We can take our eyes off the Way in many ways.*

Chris's *Uncle Dogmatic* joined a staunch, strict congregation in *Destruction City*. He often boasted about their doctrine's perfection and the strength of their faith. Apparently outward appearance was most important, making myself and others feel disparaged and slated. *Uncle Dogmatic* never showed grace or compassion, only a sense of superiority. No one from the congregation took the opportunity to share the *free gift* of eternal life through Jesus Christ.

Chris concluded; *I must never seek the praise and approval of man; never!* He understood to be in *The King's* service, he must have a servant's spirit, looking out for the needs of others.

The day ended with Christian feeling radiant. He left *Destruction City* to find hope and purpose. And now, he found it. With his sins removed **As far as the east is from the west,** *So* **far has He removed our transgressions from us.** *Psalms 103:12* Chris has been liberated.

Now, with new hope, he has confidence that his children will successfully navigate this confused and wicked world. What he has learned from The Big Book has given him wisdom, knowledge, and discernment of the visible and invisible world.

His purpose and mission are clear, **"You shall love the Lord your God with all your heart, and with all your soul, and with all your strength, and with all your mind; and love your neighbor as yourself."** *Luke 10:27*

Chris is in a good place. **Delight yourself in the Lord; And He will give you the desires of your heart.** *Psalms 37:4*

Christian laid down, covered himself, and began to snore. **In peace I will both lie down and sleep, For You alone, O LORD, make me dwell in safety.** *Psalms 4:8*

Chapter 16
Snared

A new day dawned, and Chris continued on. Snapping from his thoughts, Chris came to a fork in the path. Suddenly, he was confronted by a radiant-looking man in white. "Follow me," the man ordered.

Due to his commanding and impressive appearance, Chris meekly followed the tall man without question. He shadowed the man in white for some distance, and then a flash of horror swept over Chris as he realized a net had fallen on him. Chris was ensnared!

Thrashing and yelling in panic, he fought to no avail. The more he struggled, the more entangled he became. Finally, Chris stopped, realizing he was on the verge of passing out. Panting for air, Chris looked at the man in white who was disrobing, dropping his shawl to the ground. Looking down at him, grinning, was a vile evil creature. He laughed at Chris, taunting him for his gullibility.

Chris was so angry with himself. *So how to get out of this mess? This is what the Shepherds warned me about, The Deceiver!*

Having accomplished his mission, *The Deceiver* walked away snorting, growling, and belching puffs of smoke from its mouth. "See you later," he hissed. "And by the way, you are on the wrong path!"

Snared, Chris was trapped. He couldn't even move his arms and hands. Hours passed, and hopelessness settled over Chris. He lay motionless, weeping; his anger turned into shame. *How could I have allowed this? I know better.* Chris called out to God for deliverance, then fell asleep.

He awakened at the break of dawn with sparrows circling over. They began tearing off the cotton strands from the net for their nests. Soon there was a break in the net. Chris slipped his hand into his pocket and pulled out his knife. Slowly, he cut the net until he freed himself. Finally, he jumped up and hightailed it back to *The Way*.

When he reached the fork in the road, another one in white sat on a boulder. However, this one was genuinely bright, an Angel. He asked Chris, "Why were you ensnared?"

Dripping with embarrassment, Chris explained. "I walked off the path onto another because of *The Deceiver's* appearance and commanding voice. I didn't pause to reflect on the warnings from *The Shepherds*."

Pressing the issue, the Angel continued, "Even after *Shepherd's* warning about *Mr. Deceiver*, you fell for it? So easily deceived!" The Angel wagged his head. "Now, you must continue, and from now on, remain alert!"

Chris answered, "Yes, I will." Then he asked, "The sparrows, did you send them?"

The *Bright One* smiled, "They needed material for their nests; the sparrows must also be cared for!" Suddenly, a passage flashed on the screen of his noodle. **Are not five sparrows sold for two cents?** *Yet* **not one of them is forgotten before God.** Luke 12:6

The *Bright One* continued, "Pay attention, you are being watched, and it's only the unmerited favor of the *Master* from the *Celestial City* who charged me to rescue you. So, be careful, or the next time, there may be severe consequences."

Chris received correction, then became thankful, raising his hands towards heaven. The Angel vanished, leaving Chris on the path alone. Still dazed by the recent bizarre occurrence, Chris continued his journey.

Disgusted with his lack of judgment, Chris chastised himself. *I can't believe I fell for Mr. Smooth Talker. I considered myself wise and discerning. But looks are deceiving; this, too, is in The Big Book!* **Beware of the false prophets, who come to you in sheep's clothing, but inwardly are ravenous wolves. You will know them by their fruits.** Matthew 7:15

Chris concluded, *There's that passage again! He snookered me just like ole Worldly Wiseman did. That's it; from now on, I will draw my conclusions by what people do, not by what they say or how they look!* While Chris continued his *Walk*, he memorized passages to assure ole *Twinkle Tongue* would never prank him again!

Autumn arrived, and snow-capped mountains surrounded Chris. The countryside unveiled variegated colors of yellows, oranges, blues, and reds. Christian has matured and sees the world differently than before. More prudent, he speaks less and listens more. He cherishes the good things in life, family, the beauty of creation, and the miracle of life. Yet, although older, his path has not ended.

Coming out of the woods into a valley. He sees a sign on the left directing travelers to *Worldly University*. This triggered a red flag. This institution is world-renowned, and its present educator's roots weave back into Babylon and the tower of Babel. Over time this *worldly institution* has groomed leaders, journalists, and educators into a progressive, utopian worldview. Its tentacles of deceit begin in school boards, mayors, and town committees, up to positions in the highest places, judges, bankers, and kings.

Chris heard shouting. He looked up the trail and saw a young man running for his life. Close behind were two university officers chasing him. Finally, he reached Chris, then jumped on *The Way*. The cops dug in their heels and came to a screeching halt at *The Way's* edge.

Then, one officer scorned the young man. "If you ever step foot on these grounds again, you will be arrested and confined to our re-education camp until you come to your senses." The two officers spun around and wobbled back up the trail toward *Worldly University.*

"Who are you?" asked Chris.

Mindful, my name is *Mindful.*"

Loaded with questions, Chris said, "Let's sit over here, and you can tell me what's going on."

Next to a bench was a fountain that bubbled spring water. Christian and *Mindful* cupped their hands and drank until their thirst quenched, then sat down.

"So, why were those officers chasing you?" asked Chris.

Mindful finally calmed down and was ready to answer. "I was attending a *World Religion* class taught by *Professor Alexander Atheist.* He revealed his hostility to *The Way,* so I raised my hand and asked him who his god was. He became indignant and loudly proclaimed, 'God does not exist! I am god, and I decide what my truth is!' Then he barked, 'I'm a Professor, a Ph.D., and a world lecturer. I'm more educated and cleverer than you will ever hope to be!'

I shrank back, then asked *Professor Atheist,* 'Am I allowed to question you in a civil discussion to benefit my education? Isn't that how learning is supposed to work, with questions

Professor Atheist

and answers?' *Professor Atheist* realized he got caught preventing freedom of thought and ideas, so he reeled himself back in and told me to continue.

So, I continued. 'You do not believe that creation is the explanation for life?' *Professor Atheist* shot back, 'Of course not! I believe in science; I'm not a flat-earther!' Then I asked him, 'Isn't science just knowledge, the discovery of God's splendorous creation?' *Professor Atheist* lost control and shouted, 'No! Nothing was created; all of life resulted from a cosmic explosion, then life began and evolved!'"

Chris, now enthralled, asked, "Then what happened?"

Mindful resumed. "Determined not to be humiliated in front of his students, he allowed me to go on, confident he would grind me into dust. So, I asked him a few more common-sense questions. But first, I explained to the professor and the class the *Foundational Principle* on which science must begin, *Design* and *Order,* and that design and order could never result from an accident.

Then, I attempted to reason with them, explaining that something cannot come from nothing, excluding a divine miracle. I asked him, Please explain how our perfectly designed bodies resulted from chaos. Furthermore, how can the brilliance of our DNA, the embedded blueprint of every life form on earth, possibly result from an accident?

Next, I removed my wristwatch and raised it for everyone to see. I asked, Is there anyone here who honestly believes this watch, with all its precisely fitted gears and springs, could be the product of an accident? And do you think that the material components of this watch came from nothing?"

"Then what happened?" requested Chris.

"Well, he popped his cork! *Professor* Atheist's face turned red as he pounded on his desk, yelling, 'This is absurd, and I suppose you believe in *The Promised Land!*'

I answered, 'Yes, I do.' Then the students laughed while *Mr. Atheist* shouted, 'What a fool you are, there is no such place; this is a figment of your imagination.' Then he began yelling for the campus police. I didn't hesitate; I ran out of the class, and thank God, I made it to *The Way*

Chris remarked, "You're one brave soul confronting ole *Professor Atheist*."

Mindful told Chris that this university used to be named *Cathedral University*, started hundreds of years ago by dedicated followers of *The King*. Its purpose was to educate and prepare believers in every aspect of life to benefit society and spread the gospel. But unfortunately, impostors and fakes crept in and defiled the university and its mission over the years. So now, *Worldly University* is the antithesis of its original mission, very sad! Chris quoted a passage, "The Big Book is correct; **the fool has said in his heart, there is no God.**" Psalms 14:1

Mindful responded. "That's the truth, and that reminds me of these passages, **the wisdom of this world is foolishness with God.** 1 Corinthians 3:19 And, **Professing to be wise, they became fools.** Romans 1:22

Chris added, "The day is coming when *Professor Atheist* will learn if he professed the truth or was, indeed, **the enemy of God.** James 4:4

So, what now," asked Chris.

Mindful answered, "I'll return home to my parents for advice. So many institutions have risen, and they are fervent and determined to serve *The Holy One*."

Chris said, "Well, it looks like you've got a handle on this brother; blessings to you, and be careful."

"I will, Chris, goodbye." *Mindful* leaned down and picked up a broken branch, then strolled up the path, using it as a walking stick, and in his other hand was his Big Black Book.

Chris pondered: *It's reassuring to know young people still see the Way. Mindful has the knowledge and courage to challenge those who use their power to indoctrinate young minds.*

Chris moved on. With this latest occurrence stirring, he wrestled over the dominance of secular education, and how it has infected the minds and hearts of children. *What has happened? We have lost control of our children's education! They're being indoctrinated with the unspeakable!*

Like so many times before, passages from *The King* surfaced in Christian's mind. **Let the little children come to me, do not hinder them, for the kingdom of heaven belongs to such as these.** Matthew 19:14 *And now, parents who take a stand become targets of godless tyrannical government bullies.* **Woe to the wicked! It will go badly with him, For what he deserves will be done to him.** Isaiah 3:11

Chris concluded, *Undoubtedly, the prophecies in our King's Big Book are true.* **But realize this, that in the last days difficult times will come. For men will be lovers of self, lovers of money, boastful, arrogant, revilers, disobedient to parents, ungrateful, unholy, unloving, irreconcilable, malicious gossips, without self-control, brutal, haters of good, treacherous, reckless, conceited, lovers of pleasure rather than lovers of God.** 2 Timothy 3:1-4

Chris looked up. There, on a fallen tree, sat a raven staring at him. Then the raven jumped from the branch and flew away, cawing until it could no longer be heard. Chris watched as the raven flew off in the distance. Then it circled over *Worldly University* on top of a hill. Slowly, The raven spiraled down until it landed on the steeple to signify ownership. When Christian saw this, he shivered.

Chapter 17
The Resting Lodge

Seasons have come and gone, as have the trials, tribulations, victories, and blessings. Christian is old, his hair silver-gray, and limps. Although slower, he remained active on *The Way*. He has helped those on the path, to have a closer relationship with *The King*.

Chris recalled the first passage he memorized from his now-frayed Big Black Book. **Come to Me, all who are weary and heavy burdened, and I will give you rest. Take My yoke upon you, and learn from Me, for I am gentle and humble in heart; and you shall find rest for your souls.** Matthew 11:28

Fortunately, Chris took heed, came to Jesus, lost his burden, and received rest; but moreover, Chris faithfully sought *The Lord* and learned of Him. Over the years, he discovered that Jesus was indeed gentle and humble.

Having learned to *walk in the spirit,* Chris experienced the reality of what *The Savior* promised in The Big Black Book. **Behold, I stand at the door and knock; if anyone hears my voice and opens the door, I will come into him, and will dine with him, and he with Me.** Revelations 3:20

Chris persistently entered *The King's* presence as he worshipped, prayed, and read The Big Book. As a result, he became acutely aware of *The King's* provisions, guidance, and protection throughout his long journey. Christian was *Grateful.*

Ahead, Chris spotted a charming house where smoke drifted up from the brick chimney. Cold and fatigued, he walked to the porch and knocked on the door. While he waited, he heard the music of angels and smelled the aroma of fresh bread.

Chris perceived that the presence of *The Lord* was upon this home. The door released and slowly opened, and the face of a sweet elderly woman appeared. "Hello, what can I do for you?"

Shivering, he uttered, "Hello, ma'am, my name is Christian; I'm sorry to bother you, but I'm cold and tired and hoped to find somewhere to lodge."

The weathered, yet pleasant-looking woman said, "Have you been traveling *The Way,* beginning at the foot of *The Cross?*"

"Yes," chattered Chris.

"Come in, Christian; go to the chair and sit."

Above the chair was a painting of a sunset; he studied it. He would soon understand the significance of this beautiful piece of art. His body warmed with soothing tranquility. Coming to him, the woman introduced herself. "My name is *Lady Calming*, and yes, I have a room and plenty of food for you before you continue the last leg of your journey. So please sit and snack on a bread roll before dinner!"

Chris commented, "This is a very comfortable place!"

"Yes, it is. This home is called *The Resting Lodge* for those who have been faithful on *The Way. The King* created this dwelling for His children, nearing the end of their journey. The purpose is to bring comfort and peace while transitioning from this world to *The Promised Land.*"

Lady Calming explained further, "Many mortals fear death; some become tormented, surrounded by cold darkness. However, this transition is peaceful for those who have surrendered their lives to *The King.* Those who truly believed and trusted Him."

Chris asked, "How long have you been here, and what is your role?"

"I've been here forever, and I provide each *Wayfarer* rest and

Lady Calming

"comfort before continuing to the *River of Death*. "So, my *Walk* is nearing its end?" questioned Chris.

Yes, Christian, as you already know, your physical body has been subjected to corruption and time, leading to death. Your house will expire soon, and the real Christian will move on."

Chris referred to The Big Book. **For we know that if the earthly tent which is our house is torn down, we have a building from God, a house not made with hands, eternal in the heavens. For indeed in this house, we groan, longing to be clothed with our dwelling from heaven, inasmuch as**

we, having put it on, will not be found naked.

For indeed while we are in this tent, we groan, being burdened, because we do not want to be unclothed but to be clothed, so that what is mortal will be swallowed up by life. Now He who prepared us for this very purpose is God, who gave to us the Spirit as a pledge. *2 Corinthians 5:1-5*

"Precisely, Christian, you will receive a spiritual body that will last for eternity without pain, suffering, and decay. There will be no more sorrow and tears, only peace, joy, and love."

Lady Calming sat Chris down for dinner with the others resting in the lodge. Everyone shared stories of their journeys, humor, and harrowing tales. Most *wayfarers* were old; however, some were young, whose earthly bodies broke down rapidly from disease. Although their time on earth was short, they will exist in their new bodies in *The King's* presence for eternity.

Then, *Lady Calming* spoke up. "Chris, I must inform you that *Faithful* came here before you."

This shook Chris. "He was behind me on *The Way*, stuck in *Vanity Fair*. Do you mean he entered the *Promised Land?* What happened?"

Lady Calming answered. "Yes, he's crossed *The River of Death*. One day during re-education classes, *Faithful* spoke out. He attempted to refute the instructor's new rules, definitions, and guidelines for words and thoughts we can no longer use. And for new words, we must use instead."

"I'm not sure I understand," Chris said.

"You see, in The Big Book, *Our Creator* clearly defined a man, and a woman. There are no gray areas, and each has distinct roles, working in unison to better the family and society. His clarity on the differences is absolute.

"However, these definitions and roles have been rejected

because of man's rebellion and stubbornness, severely creating havoc with *The King's* design and the human race. Yet, over at *Worldly University,* these radical ideas are being taught. They instruct students that this is the *new norm,* and anyone who does not conform is labeled *a bigot* and *a sexist,* deserving to be shamed and punished. Students are encouraged to be *offended, indignant,* and even *unruly* with anyone who rejects their definitions concerning what a man a woman, and a family are.

"That's not all, Chris. They have intentionally divided people into groups, *racial, gender, rich,* and *poor.* This is an ancient *Satanic* tactic practiced by those who knowingly or unknowingly carry out the missions of **the god of this world.** Our King said **if a house is divided against itself, it will not stand.** Mark 3:25

"These academic elitists and corrupt politicians are self-appointed magistrates who dictate to the world what we can and cannot say. And those who resist are targeted. Because of them, people are pitted against each other, resulting in anger, hate, and violence. It's not bringing people together but only creating blame and hatred. They have become the **enemy of God.** James 4:4

"*Faithful* stood firm; he pointed out examples of confusion and chaos imposed on children, adults, families, and humanity. The instructor could not tolerate *Faithful's* comments; he called him an intolerant caveman, then had him arrested for violating his probation. *Faithful* was taken away in handcuffs, tried again before *Judge Hategood,* and sentenced to life in prison.

"The prison guards placed him with murderers, pedophiles, and gang members. He lasted only one week; then he was murdered while attempting to read The Big Book to a cellmate."

Although saddened, Chris felt tremendous anger toward those who performed this travesty. "This is evil; *Faithful* was a good and brave man!" Chris quickly opened his Big Book and read with authority. "**Woe to those who call evil good and good evil; Who substitute darkness for light and light for darkness; Who substitute bitter for sweet and sweet for bitter! Woe to those who are wise in their own eyes and clever in their own sight.**" *Isiah 5:20*

He slammed The Book shut and declared, "These people will meet a worse end than *Faithful* if they refuse to repent and come to *The Savior.*"

Lady Calming patted Chris on the shoulder. "I understand your anger; your sorrow will be brief. But, Chris, I have some news about your friend *Grateful.*"

His ears perked up. "No kidding? He went ahead of me while I spent time with my family. I never caught up with him; what happened?"

Lady Calming said, "From above, word came that *Grateful* went to the edge of a brook to rest and refresh himself with a cool drink of water. Spanning the creek was an old bridge covered with vines. *Grateful* laid back and fell asleep. When he awakened, a beautiful young maiden stood on the old bridge with skin soft as cream and long black hair. She was staring at *Grateful* with a smile. Being lonely and wanting to be polite, *Grateful* stood up, walked to the bridge, and introduced himself.

"Hi, I'm *Grateful,*" the maiden responded. "Hi, *Grateful*; my name is *Allure!*" She stretched her arm and touched *Grateful* with her small delicate hand. *Allure* locked onto *Grateful* with her large, deep blue eyes: then she asked, 'What brings you here?"

"I was walking along *The Way,* dry as a bone, thirsting for water when I saw the brook, so I stopped to drink and rest."

Lady Calming continued the story. "*Allure* had befriended many men followers on *The Way.* And, like the others, she lulled

Grateful into putty using her feminine charms. She persuaded her victims with her sweet soft voice, telling them, '*The Way* is good, but if you get carried away, that's the wrong way!' She has convinced many men that attending church once a week is enough. So, she swayed *Grateful* not to deprive himself because of something that happened thousands of years ago.

Grateful became enchanted and got sucked into a relationship with this beauty. However, it didn't take long before *Allure* exposed her deep hostility to *The Way*. Fortunately, *Grateful* broke the spell when he realized *Allure* was forcing him to choose her over *The Savior*. He jumped up and sprinted back to *The Way*. As *Grateful* ran up the path, he heard screams of profanities echoing through the woods, coming from this pretty—little package. *Grateful* wasted a lot of time and was nearly compromised for the remainder of his days."

Chris asked. "So, he's on *The Way* now?

"*Lady Calming* answered, "Yes!"

Then Chris shared with the group a similar incident that happened to *Faithful*. A shameless, brazen married woman named *Wantona* nearly destroyed his *Walk*.

"Yes, Christian, that's the number one stumbling block for men. And there is no question the *Evil One* uses this intoxicating appetite to pull men into the *Dark Caverns of Lust*. The ramifications are deep and wide and have changed the course of individuals, marriages, families, and nations. Oh, that men would heed the warnings in The Big Book. **Flee immorality, Every *other* sin that a man commits is outside the body, but the immoral man sins against his own body. Or do you not know that your body is a temple of the Holy Spirit who is in you, whom you have from God, and that you are not your own? For you have been bought with a price: therefore, glorify God in your body.** *1 Corinthians 6:18-20*

Now get to bed, Chris; you'll leave in the morning. Hopefully, *Grateful* will catch up with you soon."

Chris rose from his chair, embraced *Lady Calming*, and went to bed.

Awakened to a new day, Chris looked out the bedroom window. The rays of sunbeams broke through the snow-blanket pines. A deer and her fawns walked through the snow, searching for food. Chris paused to thank God for His many unique creations. Then, he entered the dining room, where *Lady Calming* had breakfast waiting.

"Good morning, Chris; I take it you slept well?"

Chris answered, "I sure did, and I feel twenty years younger!"

"Settle down Chris," *Lady Calming* joked.

They bowed their heads, and Chris thanked *The Lord* for His goodness. Then, they savored the moment in their last meal together. Afterward, *Lady Calming* took Chris aside and asked, "So, how are you feeling right now?"

Chris answered honestly. "For so long, I have studied and spoken of my *Lord's Kingdom,* yet crossing the *River of Death* makes me apprehensive."

"Chris, I understand; however, take heart that when the time comes, it will be peaceful. Be encouraged; I know what has been written in your book thus far. You became a priest for your family and walked through life with integrity. Your family, friends, and neighbors have watched. You loved your wife as Christ loved you. It's also recorded that you introduced many to *The King* and encouraged those along *The Way.* Rewards are awaiting you, beginning with **the Crown of Life!**" *James 1;12*

Calmed and assured, Chris rose. "It's time to move on." He embraced everyone and said, "We'll see each other soon!"

They all knew that time was short, putting a perspective on

relationships and time into a different domain, a sweet and pleasant moment.

Lastly, Chris thanked *Lady Calming*. They hugged, then he walked out the front door onto the path. *Lady Calming* gave Chris a heavy fur jacket, thick wool socks, and new boots. The pockets were filled with various foods and a loaf of bread. He was now prepared for the remainder of his journey.

Chapter 18
And May Enter

Months passed as Chris plodded toward his final destination. Not in such a hurry these days, he took the time to help others along his journey. Christian gave them food and water, in addition to *Comfort* and *Guidance*. It was as though he became the twin of everyone who helped him along *The Way*.

Rapidly coming up on Chris from behind was an elderly thin man with long gray hair in a ponytail. He fast-walked past Chris; it was none other than *Mr. Ignorant,* whom he had encountered years before.

Chris yelled, "Hey, *Mr. Ignorant,* slow down!"

Chris caught up with him and asked, "How have you been!"

Mr. Ignorant responded with the same tinge of pride as before. "I'm doing great, and I will enter the *Promised Land* just like I told you the first time we met. I see you're still toting that Big Black Book!"

"Yes," answered Chris. "I still refer to it whenever I need direction, help, or comfort."

Ignorant could not contain himself, so he launched a verbal arrow at Chris. "So, it's like a crutch or a security blanket, right?"

Chris gave *Mr. Ignorant* what he wanted; he conceded and agreed. "You're right, *Mr. Ignorant.* I need Him when I'm weak, grieving, discouraged, and confused; however, it works!" Chris recalled, "The last time we spoke; you said there were many ways to the *Gate of The Promised Land*. And I plead with you, *Mr. Ignorant,* please heed what it says in my tattered Big Black

Book." **For there is one God, and one mediator between God and men, the man Christ Jesus, who gave Himself as a ransom for all.** *1 Timothy 1:5*

Mr. Ignorant countered with the same retort. "As I told you many years ago, you put too much faith in that book. The Old Book is outdated and open to each person's interpretation. It's intolerant and dogmatic to claim Jesus is the only way. You're the one who should worry!"

Bewildered by *Ignorant's* spin, Chris said, "I will pray for you."

Offended by that remark, *Ignorant* replied, "Don't waste your breath." Then he hurried onward.

Chris was reminded of a proverb from The Book. **The wisdom of the wise is to understand his way, But the foolishness of fools is deceit.** *Proverbs 14:8*

Traveling on, Chris felt a change in the atmosphere. The air was clear and pure. The rivers and streams glistened. He walked through gardens displaying the most brilliant colors he had ever seen. The orchards flaunted purple plums, bright oranges, and red apples. Weaved throughout were bands of cherry trees standing on rolling carpets of strawberry patches. The meadows swirled around the trees and shrubs, exhibiting waves of greens, yellows, and lavenders as they swayed in the wind.

This plot of land was called *Farewell Estates*. This peaceful parcel provided time for the families of loved ones who were soon to finish their journey. This extraordinary place featured food, fellowship, and relaxation. However, most important, it is a safe place where loved ones can tie up loose ends and say farewell. Beautiful families mingle in and out of the fields, refreshing themselves. Others sat at round tables, saying things they wished they had said. The countryside is picturesque, and the skies reflect the significance of this precious brief moment with a mixture of sadness, tenderness, and joy. Voices are mixed with tears. Thoughts are expressed that were held back due to pride, anger, bitterness, and hurt. Whispers of "I love you," "Please forgive me," and "Thank you for caring for me" are just some of the final words spoken on this *consecrated* plot of land.

Christian decided to roam around, getting to know these gracious, loving children of *The King*. He asked if anyone had seen *Grateful,* but no one responded. Chris picked some fruit from the trees, then sat on a bench near a waterfall. While eating a ripened peach, he opened his Big Black Book for the last time. Like so many times before, it seemed as though a ministering spirit determined which page would be opened.

Chris's eyes locked on to a passage, then with a faint voice, he read to himself. **"The time of my departure has come. I have fought the good fight, I have finished the course, I have kept the faith; in the future, there is laid up for me the crown of righteousness, which the Lord, the righteous Judge will award to me on that day; and not only me, but also to all who have loved His appearing."** *2 Timothy 4:6-8*

Chris straightened his back, took a deep breath, then began to weep. While wiping his tears, he gazed across the meadow. He noticed a lion sitting majestically on a tall boulder, looking over the valley. Not sure what to make of it, he searched his memory about a Lion in *The Big Book.* Then it came to him. *The Lion of Judah, that's it; he must be the Lion of Judah from the book of Revelations! So, HE is here protecting His own!*

Enthralled with the majesty of this Lion, Christian was unaware of Angela and his family standing behind him. But then, Chris felt their presence and stood up slowly. Overwhelmed, everyone wept and came together in a family hug.

Daniel Says Goodbye

Like the other families surrounding them, they resolved unforgiveness and bitterness.

But what was expressed chiefly was, "I love you!"

Chris encouraged his family to remain faithful, diligent, and upright. Then he assured them. "Although we will be apart, take heart; we will come together again."

The family sat in a site reserved for them. They talked, reminisced, laughed, and cried. Chris placed his grandson, Daniel, on his lap and hugged him. He whispered to Daniel,

"This is what the Lord requires of you, to do justice, to love kindness, and to walk humbly with your God." Micah 6:8

Chris planted a seed in Daniel's heart that directed the course of his life. Daniel will become a pillar of strength; he will refuse to be a friend of this world. Daniel will become a man of God.

Knowing the magnitude of this moment, this tender young boy wept.

Then Chris told the love of his life, Angela, "I love you."

Chris sensed a tugging telling him it was time to move on. He gave his Big Black Book to Daniel, then kissed him on the forehead. The family engaged in final hugs and tears, then he turned around and walked back to the path.

Angela and the family remained seated as they watched their patriarch disappear over the hill. They sat silently, engulfed in tears of sadness, expressions of joy, **and the peace of God which surpasses all comprehension.** Philippians 4:7

Christian caught his breath and began his final ascent. Then, at last, he reached the top and stopped; he looked below and saw the *River of Death*. Chris paused, then sat down in the *Chair of Reflection*.

I've had a good long life, thank you, Lord. His thoughts were those of gratitude for his family, friends, and the many experiences throughout his life.

Then Chris saw two people climbing the trail. Finally, they got close enough to recognize each other. It was *Grateful* and *Joy*.

Chris stood and began waving his arms. When they reached the top, they embraced. Unexpectedly, two more chairs appeared, so they sat and talked. Chris remarked, "This is incredible; I thought you would never catch up with me."

Grateful spoke, "If it weren't for my fiasco with *Allure,* I would have arrived sooner; however, later on, *Joy* and I met on the path and fell in love. We've been married for sixty years and have followed *The Way* together. Now it looks like we will cross that *River* together."

Joy looked up at *Grateful* with admiration, then said, "We both lived in *Vanity Fair* for many years and knew each other from childhood. But, because of you and *Faithful*, we, too, are on *The Way*. Shortly after leaving me at the safe house with *Comfort* and *Guidance*, I heard about *Faithful's* tragic death. I was indebted to you and *Faithful*; it tore me apart. I stayed with *Comfort* and *Guidance* until I gave birth to a baby boy; I named him *Faithful*."

Chris became emotional. "Then what happened?"

Joy explained. "As soon as the baby was ready, I thanked *Comfort* and *Guidance*, then began on *The Way*, hoping to find you. I wanted to tell you about *Faithful*; instead, I found *Grateful*."

Both smiled, then kissed. *Grateful* told Chris that he adopted *Joy's* son and raised him in *The Way*. "When he became a young man, he returned to the outskirts of *Vanity Fair* to help *Comfort* and *Guidance*. Our son *Faithful* continued their work when they passed on.

Chris saw that they were proud of their son, and he was happy for them. Then, silence settled over them while they stared at the *River of Death* below. Then Christian announced, "It's time!"

They stood from their chairs and walked down the hill. When they reached the edge of the *River of Death*, Chris took off his shoes and stepped into the dark water. "Whoa, that's cold!"

Joy became fearful, doubting she wouldn't make it through *The Gate*. "My life has been a mess, and I've made some real blunders throughout my journey."

Grateful encouraged her. "Come on, *Joy*, don't be afraid. His love and mercy will get us to the other side. Look up; you can see *The City*!"

Joy embraced *Grateful*. They held hands and looked to the other side, where a continuous blaze of light flashed into the heavens. Suddenly, two *Bright Ones* appeared, two men in golden apparel. They laid their hands on them and whispered, "Step in!"

Christian, *Grateful*, and *Joy* stepped into the river together; the crossing happened in the blink of an eye. Standing on the other side of the *River of Death*, Chris, *Grateful*, and *Joy* stood wide-eyed, looking at their new bodies. First, they felt weightless, then realized the *River of Death* had swallowed up their earthly bodies. This fulfilled the promise from The Big Book. **For this corruptible must put on incorruption, and this mortal must put on immortality.** 1 Corinthians 15:53

They were clothed with robes of white, and they spoke the language of angels. Then, with the *Bright Ones* still at their side, they began up the hill to *The Celestial City's Gate*. Noticeable was the ease they experienced when walking upward. They had never felt this condition before. It was magnificent!

The Shining Ones briefed Christian, *Joy*, and *Grateful*. "When you enter *The City*, you will never know again sin, sorrow, disease, and heartache. Instead, there will be joy and peace like you've never known."

"Yes," said the other *Shining One*. "You will be rewarded for the suffering you endured for *His Name*. And, for your tears and prayers. Rewards for loving your enemies, and rewards for your generosity."

Then the other *Shining One* continued. "You'll join your loved ones and old friends who came to *The Celestial City* before you. You will meet the saints of God throughout eternity. However, the greatest ever will be when you meet, *The Good Shepherd*,

The King of Kings, The Lamb of God, The Prince of Peace, The Word of God, and The Mighty God.

You will come face to face with *The Savior, Jesus Christ.*"

This overwhelmed Christian, *Joy,* and *Grateful;* they hungered for what would happen once they entered *The Gate.*

Nearing the top, Christian looked to the left; he saw *Mr. Ignorant* being escorted away from *The Celestial City* on a rocky trail into the darkness beyond. Red eruptions rolled upward from the deep canyons reflecting off the black clouds above. Finally, *Ignorant* disappeared into eternity. Christian watched; this would be the last bout with sadness he would ever experience.

They reached the top, the trumpet sounded, and *The Gate* opened. A congregation of people swarmed around to meet them. Christian, *Joy,* and *Grateful* recognized many. Among them stood *Faithful;* they came together and embraced.

Then, a glorious presentation. Angelic hosts awarded each one: **The Crown of Life,** *Revelations 2:10* **The Crown of Glory,** *1 Peter 5: 4* and, **The Crown of Righteousness.** *2 Timothy 4:8*

There was laughter, rejoicing, and an overwhelming feeling of love that surrounded everyone. There were voices, loving voices. There was a touch, a tender touch.

Above, *The Gate* was an inscription in *Gold.*

BLESSED ARE THEY WHO DO HIS COMMANDMENTS, THAT THEY MAY HAVE RIGHT TO THE TREE OF LIFE AND MAY ENTER IN THROUGH THE GATE INTO THE CITY. *Revelation 22:14*

Christian, *Joy,* and *Grateful* passed through the portals of the shining *Gate* into the *Celestial City* and witnessed a panorama that no mortal could ever define with words or illustrations.

The End

Thank you for reading
Christian's Walk ~ The Journey

I trust this book has blessed you. I intended to create a means to introduce The Savior to a confused and lost world. And to invigorate The King's children to fulfill their purpose, making the most of their time.

Please put this book into the hands of family, friends, and acquaintances. Let's see if we can grow His kingdom!

Write me at: myvietnam1949@gmail.com
Visit my website: myvietnambook.com
https://www.facebook.com/JackAllenBillups

Outstanding Memoir

My Vietnam: A Gift to My Daughter is truly a gift to all Americans, but especially for all those who who have served. Jack Billups has truly written a masterpiece of "the Grunt" experience in Vietnam. A book that should be required reading throughout academia and our secondary schools so that current and future generations will truly understand the consequences of decisions made by our political leaders. My Vietnam is a true tribute to those that served in Vietnam and especially to those who made the ultimate sacrifice. Let them never be forgotten. Show Less

Shopper name: Scott R.

myvietnambook.com

Printed in the USA
CPSIA information can be obtained
at www.ICGtesting.com
JSHW021115111023
49929JS00003B/103

9 781736 037669